CARTWHEELS IN THE DARK

Karla Jordan

This book is dedicated to my grandmother, Doris Irene Worthley. I knew her as simply, "Nana." She was the most selfless, loving, caring woman I have ever known. Nana, I heard your message loud and clear and I did not quit. This is for and because of you.

A NOTE FROM THE AUTHOR

I hope you enjoy my debut book! I would love to hear your thoughts once you have finished reading "Cartwheels in The Dark."

Please consider going to Amazon and leaving a review. Reviews are so important to authors, especially first-time authors.

I can also be contacted at Goodreads, Instagram, Twitter, Facebook and as always, through my website. I look forward to hearing from you!

karlajordan-author.com

ACKNOWLEDGMENTS

First, I want to thank Carlton Worthley, also known as my Dad. Without the love and support of you throughout my entire life, I surely would not be putting forth a book to share with others. Thank you, Dad, for all you have done and continue to do, for your daughters and everyone and anyone that ever needs a helping hand. I am the person I am because of you, and as much as I love words, I will never be able to find the right ones to accurately express how much you mean to me. I would also like to thank my late mother, Jean, for showing me how to never give up. I watched her latch on to an idea and not let go. I thank you, Mum, for your strength because you made me a stronger woman.

To my husband, Dana, who has listened to more of this story and the publishing business than I'm sure he ever cared to,but listened to me go on and on just the same. Thank you for supporting my dream.

Thank you to my "unofficial editor" Cathe. The hours and hours of sending emails back and forth to get it "just right," I appreciated so much more than you know. Your friendship means the world!

To all my family and friends who have shown me support for this book, I thank you for your friendship and support. You will never know how much you mean to me. Your encouragement and support mean the world to me. I would especially like to thank Mary and Robinfor not letting me put this manuscript on a shelf again. I am truly grateful for all of you.

I also want to thank my high school English teachers who pushed me to be the best writer I could be. They refused to let me settle for "good enough" when they knew that I do it "right" with a little bit of effort.

REVIEWS FROM READERS

"Congratulations for a wonderful debut novel! I thoroughly enjoyed it. Right from the beginning, the prologue grabs you and before you know it, you are deeply involved in the story. There's also a nice twist or two, but I won't spoil that for other readers. Very beautifully written and smooth story...just the kind of book I love! Can't wait for the next one!"
C.K. Calgary, Alberta, Canada

"As an avid reader, I absolutely loved this book! Fast paced and kept my interest! I can't wait to read the next book by Karla Jordan!"
M.P. Maine

"I absolutely LOVE this book! I could not put it down! The story completely captivated me and I couldn't wait to see what happened next for Kallie. I look forward to Karla Jordan's next book!"
K.P. Florida

PROLOGUE

Somerfield, Maine 1975

A single bulb hanging from the splintered old rafter cast a dim light inside of the rickety woodshed. The air was thick with heavy earthy smells that come from days of damp rain and not so much as a drop of sunshine. The fog had swallowed up every inch of ground not covered by trees, and they too were partially lost in the mist.

The sound of metal hitting rock, attempting to slice through hard patches of ground laced with gnarled tree roots, filled the air. A moment of silence and then again-the echoes of metal against rock. Over and over again until there were no more sounds. No sounds at all. No night bird songs. No crickets. Nothing but the sound of a distant owl hooting, to break the silence.

From behind the trunk of the giant maple tree, I stood completely still. In my worn-out nightgown and bare feet, I stood as quietly as I could and waited. With no idea what I was waiting for, something in my bones told me to stay out of sight. A game of hide and seek except there was no game. This was real.

The creaking of the shed door opening startled me. My fingers dug into the deep creases in the bark of the tree as I steadied myself and strained to see through the darkness and the fog. Someone was out there in the woodshed. But who? And why?

It was the middle of the night, and the house was quiet. The other children had been asleep for hours now. I should have been too. I would have been if not for the sounds of dead branches hitting against the thin pane of the bedroom window each time the wind blew. Like a message of Morse Code, the tapping had been enough to wake me. It was only then that I heard the noises outside-the metal grinding against rock. Curiosity got the better of me and I crept outside to see what was going on. Half of me knew that I should not have been there behind that tree. The other half dying to know what was going on out there in the middle of the night. I should have stayed in bed. I shouldn't have stuck my nose where it didn't belong. Only it was too late for that now. I was there in the shadows hoping to discover something, though I had no idea what.

As my eyes adjusted to the darkness of the night, I saw it. I strained to see clearer, just to be sure but there was no mistaking what was there in front of me. The outline of a body, face up to the night sky, still and not moving. It was a body all right. I didn't want it to be, but it was. I closed my eyes and counted to ten as though somehow, magically, that would make it disappear.

I brushed the strands of hair that had become dampened by the mist, from my eyes. Slowly, I opened one eye and then the other. It hadn't been an illusion created by the fog or by my overactive imagination. No. It was real. Closing my eyes wasn't going to make it not be so. A body was lying there on the ground in front of the woodshed, perfectly still.

All at once I knew I had to run. Fast. Without looking back, I ran for the safety of the front door to the shack and flew to my bed, my feet barely touching the floor as I ran. Through the shoddy walls of the house, I could hear them-the heavy footsteps coming closer to the bedroom window. I threw the ratty quilt over my head and held my breath.

CHAPTER ONE

Vienna, Virginia 1997

Staring vacantly out the small window beside her, Kallie watched the wispy thin fast-moving clouds pass by and wondered if Maddie had ever seen the view from so high above the earth. Somehow, she doubted it. The older woman always said she had everything she wanted or needed right there in her small town of Bradford, Maine and had no desire to travel anywhere else. She smiled as she remembered how genuinely kind and caring Maddie had been to her from the very first time she met her.

What she must have thought about the barefoot ragamuffin child sitting alone on a park bench, at the edge of darkness with nothing but a well-worn suitcase beside her. Kallie hadn't thought of that day in what seemed like forever. It wasn't something she cared to remember. Her entire childhood before she met Maddie was something she would rather forget. It had been tucked away in that place where people put things they don't want to remember. Sometimes just for a while. Sometimes forever. For Kallie it had been thirty years. It had been then that she left Kahlua Jansen behind and didn't look back for a single second.

Not that there was anything to look back for. A childhood riddled with poverty and two alcoholic parents wasn't something she chose to revisit. After the life they had given her, Kallie couldn't care less if they were doing well or six feet under. From the time she had learned to read and saw her *name* on an empty liquor bottle she'd found lying under the kitchen table, she realized her parents weren't the kind of people she was ever going to have an ounce of respect for. They hadn't proved her wrong.

She did think about her younger sisters from time to time, though. But never her parents. She hoped the girls had grown into successful, happy people but she also knew the odds were not in their favor. None of them had been handed anything resembling a normal childhood. Still, she hoped they had found happiness somewhere along the way, as she had with Maddie.

Her childhood home had been nothing more than a shack, that truth be known, was better suited for farm animals and had more than likely been meant for that purpose, originally. Wooden splintered shingles hung loosely from the sides of the building. Some dangled by the head of a single rusted nail. Others had rotted completely and fallen to the ground in spongy slivers.

Inside the shack, daylight seeped in through holes in the walls. Light and air pushed through the aged rough-cut floors, providing a year-round ventilation system. In the winter, icy air would dance around bare feet brave enough to land on the planks. Snowdrifts often collected in piles around the kitchen where a good Nor'easter wind left its mark behind.

The only source of heat had been a small pot belly stove in the kitchen. The tiny cast iron barrel barely threw enough heat to warm the one room, let alone the entire shack. The water pipes froze every winter and running water was a luxury during the long winter months in Maine. Once the water froze, it wouldn't run again until spring. Even when there was running water, it was always cold. Hot water came from pots heated on the tiny wood stove.

The cupboards were all but empty most of the time. Every so often the government would issue surplus food to the poorer families in town. The children ate well during those days and not so well the rest of the time. Government cheese day was more of a special occasion than Christmas around their place. Regular meals were few and far between. For that reason, they quickly learned to eat what was on their plates. After supper one evening, Kallie had gone out to the shed for an armload of wood as her mother had yelled for her to do. As soon as she opened the door, she'd come face to face with a small animal carcass hanging from the rafter in front of her. The pelt of a racoon still hung half attached to the dinner she had just eaten. She realized then; it was best not to ask questions about what was on her plate. Food is food when you're hungry enough.

And then there was the constant arguing and fighting between her parents who stayed drunk more than they were sober. If the girls were lucky, they would beat on each other and leave the kids alone. That wasn't always the case.

No. Kallie had absolutely no reason to want to remember or relive a childhood that would only conjure up painful memories. She had buried as much as she could from that life, a long, long time ago. She was happy to leave them dead…indefinitely. To some people, she knew that would sound cold and uncaring. Until they had walked in her shoes and lived a life like she had, she didn't give a tinker's damn what anyone thought about her decision to not acknowledge those people. Maddie was her family and that's all she needed and wanted.

The day she met Madeline O'Brien had been both the best and the worst day of her life. Her mother, Connie, was drunk which was the case more often than not, the usual kind of day. Her father was nowhere to be seen, but that *wasn't* unusual. He was only ever around long enough for Connie to share whatever booze they could squeeze from the monthly welfare check. After that, he disappeared. Sure enough though, when the first of the month came back around, so did Albert Jansen out from under whatever rock he had been lying beneath since the previous months binge.

Kallie had been playing outside with her sisters for most of the day. It was a beautiful July day in Maine. She and her sisters knew the drill. They were well rehearsed at playing outside and keeping out of their mother's way. Kallie was alone reading under a shade tree when she saw the door of the shack fly open with force. Out stepped a very wobbling Connie with a stick in her hand. She marched like she was on a mission. Kallie had seen that look on her mother's face one too many times to not recognize what was about to happen. Someone was getting a whooping for something they had done. Connie headed straight for her! She thought fast trying to figure out what she could have done to warrant the determination and rage in her mother's steps. Before she knew what was happening, her mother grabbed her arm and shook her back and forth like a rag doll.

"Kahlua! Kahlua! Ya hearin' me girl? Go! Get in the car and wait for me! Do it NOW!"

"Why Mama? Where are we going?" she asked not knowing what was happening.

"Get ya ass into that car, or I'll show ya why! Ya hear me? Now, get in the frigging car and do it NOW!" Connie bellowed.

She knew better than to argue with her mother. Especially when she already had a stick in her hand and smelled like she had bathed in cheap liquor. Wherever she was going and whatever the reason, it couldn't be anything she was going to like. That much she knew for sure. There hadn't even been time to find her sneakers that were somewhere out in the yard, but she was too afraid to go back and look for them.

Kallie sat fidgeting in the front seat of the car, nervously shifting her tattered old book in her hands. Connie had gone back inside the shack but not before she yelled for her to "stay her ass right there and to not move so much as a god forsaken muscle!" It seemed like forever before her mother came back out of the shack and headed for the car. Her youngest sister, Amaretta, came running toward the car with Ginger not far behind.

"We wanna come too!" they wailed but Connie wasn't having

any of it. She swatted both of their behinds with the stick until they wailed and told them to get in the house and stay there. Her sister, Brandy, who should be watching the little ones while Connie was gone, was nowhere in sight. It was only Kahlua who was going for a ride and that was that.

Her mother drove in silence, sucking on one cigarette after another as they drove down the dusty dirt roads. As they passed Blackwater Brook, where they often swam and had bathed in, on more than one occasion, Kallie recognized where she was. They were heading for town. But why? It wasn't the first of the month, which meant that her mother wasn't heading to buy alcohol. And if she were, she would have left Kahlua home as she always did. She couldn't remember a time when she was the only one going anywhere with her mother. She wished she felt good that she'd been singled out. She wished she could have felt special that she got to go and no one else did. But she could tell by the look on her mother's face and the way she was furiously puffing on one cigarette after another, that this was not a special occasion. She didn't know what it was, but something good it wasn't. She knew Connie Jansen well enough to know that.

They were driving on pavement now and headed straight for the center of Bradford. Somerfield was too small to have it's own center of town and reaching the pavement brought them smack dab into downtown Bradford. What there was of it, anyway. There was a post office, a gas station, library, and a general store all within one hundred feet of one another. That was "town."

The car pulled up to the general store and Connie turned off the ignition. After a minute of silently chewing at her bottom lip and blowing clouds of smoke into the air, she tossed a half-smoked butt out the window and looked in Kallie's direction.

"Okay. That's that! Time to get out." she said.

"What? Mama, what do you mean?"

"I told ya to get out of the damned car, now go!" her mother barked.

Kahlua didn't understand what she was supposed to be doing. Where was she going?

"Where am I going, Mama? I don't know what you mean."

"No. Course ya don't know what I mean. Ya never was too bright I'll say that for ya!" she barked.

Connie got out of the car, opened the door to the back and took out a suitcase that looked like it had been run over quite a few times before being rescued from the town dump, which it more than likely had. The plastic handle was only half there and there were grapefruit sized holes scattered throughout the tan tweed fabric. She walked around the car, flew open the passenger door and motioned for Kahlua to get out. She did as she was told. She knew all too well the consequences for not obeying her mother. The suitcase thrust into her hands as she was ordered to sit on the bench outside the store.

"Mama what am I doing? Why do I have to sit here? Why do I have a suitcase? Where am I going?" she asked through the tears that were stinging beneath her eyelids.

Connie walked up close to her and bent down until she was eye to eye with Kahlua. "See, little girl, here's the thing. I don't care where ya goin'! Ya ARE goin' and that's all I friggin' care about at this point! And don't be callin' me Mama no more. I ain't ya Mama no more girl! Ya go now and find ya'self somebody else dumb enough for the job. It ain't me no more! I've had about all I can take of ya and I'm sick of lookin' at ya! That clear enough?"

"But what'd I do, Mama?" Kallie asked, trying to swallow the hard lump caught in her throat.

Connie looked at her with a look of disgust as though her oldest child was nothing more than a sack of trash. "I don't owe ya nothin'! And I sure as hell ain't gonna stand here and explain myself to a friggin' snot nosed kid!"

She watched as her mother ran back to the car and drove off out of sight. Connie was beyond angry at her, that much was apparent. What wasn't clear was why. What could she have done to make her mother leave her alone and tell her to go away and find another mother? People didn't just dump their children off on a bench and not come back. Did they? Kahlua watched the day end as the sun began to go down. Her mother would drive up the road and come back. She had to. Parents didn't drive off to leave their ten-year-old daughters alone after dark. Did they?

She shivered and wiped the dirty tears from her eyes. Other mothers didn't do that, she was sure. Connie was another story. Deep in her heart, she knew no one would be coming for her. What was she supposed to do? Where was she supposed to go? She was ten years old and not old enough to take care of herself. Kahlua buried her head in her hands and cried. She didn't want to, and she tried not to. She tried to be brave, but she was more scared than she'd ever been in her life! What would she do when it was pitch dark outside? There were animals that came out after dark. What if something tried to get her? Where would she run to?

She laid her head on the suitcase and sobbed until there were no more tears. She lifted her head to see an elderly woman walking toward her, but she didn't know who she was. The woman asked where her parents were. Kahlua shared what had happened and the woman took her by the hand into the general store. She led her into the rest room and told her to wash her face and when she was finished, she'd find the woman at the front of the store.

When Kahlua came out of the rest room, she could hear the woman's voice talking loudly. She was on the store's telephone telling someone that "this is not acceptable" followed by "what kind of monster are you?" She knew the woman must be talking to her mother. Had she had figured out what was going on and had sorted it all out for her? Yes! That had to be what was going on! Her mother would be coming back for her any minute now. Things would be okay soon.

When the woman hung up the phone, Kahlua was expecting her to say that everything had been sorted out and that she would be going home soon. That was not the case. The woman, who turned out to be Madeline O'Brien, was heartbroken and angry at the same time. She explained as best as she knew how to a young child, that her mother was not coming for her. She told Kahlua that she would love it if she came home with her and stayed for a while.

All Kahlua wanted to do though was go back home and crawl into the rusted old metal bed she shared with Ginger, Amaretta and Brandy. She didn't even care if there was never enough room in the bed, or that someone was always hogging the blankets. She just wanted to go home. The older woman seemed nice enough. Dressed in a yellow house dress with a knit sweater thrown across her shoulders. She reminded her of Ms. True, who had been her schoolteacher last year. But it wasn't Ms. True, and she didn't know this woman. Kallie just wanted to go home but she had no choice. That choice had been made for her. Her mother wasn't coming to get her. That was apparent. She had no choice but to trust the woman who had her by the hand, leading her to her new home up the street.

CHAPTER TWO

The pilot's voice filled the cabin to announce that they were about an hour from the Portland Jetport. Kallie couldn't believe she was really sitting on a plane, heading back to the one place she had vowed to never return. If it weren't for Maddie, she wouldn't be returning at all. Ever.

It had been only a few short hours earlier when she had seen the obituary for Madeline O'Brien in the online morning edition of the *Herald*. She had dropped and shattered the coffee mug she had been holding when she saw the unmistakable photo of the elderly woman who had taken her in so long ago. Wracked with guilt for not making more time to visit with Maddie, she found herself regretting that she had let time get away from her. She had meant to visit with her more often but there always seemed to be something going on in her life that had prevented a trip back. The more she thought about it, she realized that wasn't true. The truth was that she could have gone back to see Maddie anytime she wanted to, but she hadn't. She always felt like the reason she would not go back to Maine to visit was an unspoken thing between the two of them. She had no desire to run into Connie or Albert and although they never talked about it, Kallie always felt that Maddie understood that.

Still, now that Maddie was gone, there was a heavy guilt in the pit of her stomach that she knew she would be carrying with her for a long time. Maddie had been nothing but good to her. She had taken her in and raised her like she was her own child. She had shown her what it means to be loved unconditionally from the moment she'd taken her in. Kallie knew, without question, that she never would have amounted to a hill of beans if not for that woman. She knew she never would have made it to college. She never would have met Cam. She would not be living in a beautiful home in Virginia. She never would have had an opportunity to give back and the homeless youth at the shelter she started in Washington D.C. No. None of that would have been possible without Maddie.

After seeing the obituary, Kallie was curious as to why it had run in a Virginia newspaper. After a bit of detective work and research online, she found the attorney from Maine who had placed the obituary in the *Herald.* Attorney Miller explained that Madeline retained him a few months earlier to take care of her financial affairs upon her death. She had been adamant that he was to make sure that her photo and her brief obituary ran in every major paper in Virginia, including online editions.

She had recently been diagnosed with Stage 4 breast cancer and wanted to be sure that her "daughter" knew of her passing. Kallie was to oversee the estate and would need to meet with Attorney Miller as soon as she could get away. There was a memorial service to plan and a house that would need selling. Not to mention a lifetime of items that filled the house that would need packing and either sold or donated.

After a much-needed cry for the woman who had been so good to her and taught her all that she knew about life and love, she picked up the phone and got on the next flight to Maine. She always said it would be an icy day in hell before she ever went back but this was something that needed to be done. The closer she got to Maine, the more the storm in her gut began to rumble.

There was no doubt, whatsoever, that going back would be an uncomfortable thing to do. She wondered if it wasn't the hardest thing she'd ever do. Could she manage to avoid the poison that was Connie and Albert Jansen? They were bound to still be there. Where else could they be? If they hadn't managed to kill one another in one of their drunken rages, they would be there. They hadn't a pot to piss in or a window to throw it out, the last time Kallie knew. She doubted much had changed since then.

Kallie's plan was to meet with Attorney Miller, plan a service for Maddie, put the house up for sale and go back home. It could be that easy, couldn't it?

It would have been a whole lot less stressful if Cam had been able to come with her. But he had left that morning for London on a three weeklong business trip. He had been working day and night for the past six months to acquire an extraordinarily successful advertising agency in the UK. He was like a kid at Christmas as he packed that morning. As much as she had wanted to take him up on his offer to come along with her to Maine, she knew she couldn't ask him to do that. He had worked so hard for this acquisition, and she wasn't going to do anything to take away from that. It was important for him, and she was both proud of and happy for him. His work was what children are for some folks. Kallie's work at the shelter meant the same for her so she completely understood the importance of her husband closing that deal.

Right from the very beginning of their relationship back at Mt. Vernon University, they had discussed having children and, in the end, agreed that children would not be in either of their futures. They both had reasons for not wanting to bring children into the world, but the agreement had been the same. Cameron was an only child that was far more interested in seeing how far he could go in the advertising world. A child would have been something he knew he would end up resenting and he didn't want that. He worked extremely hard to start his advertising agency in D.C. and twenty years later, Douglas Enterprises Inc. was one of the most successful in the country. That was his baby. He didn't need or want a child that would take time away from what he really wanted to do.

Kallie had her reasons also, although different from Cam's. Deep seated memories, which were more like nightmares, of two alcoholic people who should have done anything in life but become parents, had helped to form her decision to never have children of her own, a long time ago. What did she know about raising a kid? Her role models were screaming, arguing drunks dodging coffee cups and dinner plates. For fear of ever becoming like them for a single second, she'd opted to avoid the parenting thing.

After college, she had done what she set out to do and she loved her work at the youth center. Those were her kids. She didn't need children of her own, she was giving her time and attention to kids who would otherwise be running the streets and living in cardboard boxes. There were more than enough kids who needed her help, she didn't need to give birth to any of her own. Their life together was complete just the way it was. Not that it had always been easy, nothing ever is. They went through the same difficulties that all couples go through early on in a relationship, but they had become so much stronger for it.

Cam was a good man who showed her the kind of love, respect, and support that she had not known existed until Maddie. His upbringing had been one that was completely different than her own. He lived in a charming home in a great neighborhood of Virginia. His father was an engineer who worked for Jackson Aeronautical in D.C. And though his father worked much of the time, Cam always knew, without question, that his dad loved and supported him. His mother worked as a librarian, and she also gave him the love and support that a child needs. When he shared stories from his childhood of holidays or birthday parties, Kallie tried to imagine herself in that world. Until she was ten years old, she had never known a life where a birthday was something to celebrate with a cake and presents. Nor did she know what a Christmas with gifts purchased from a store was like.

As an only child, Cam grew up blessed by the kind of life most children can only dream of. He hadn't grown up spoiled or arrogant because of his parents' privileges though. His parents had made sure of that. He learned to work hard at an early age for what he wanted in life. The fact that he could have been handed whatever he wanted, didn't matter. His parents taught him the value of goals and demanding work. That drive hadn't changed with age. He was still working hard and always challenging himself. Kallie loved that about him. If he didn't know how to do something, he would find someone to teach him or he would jump in and figure it out on his own.

She smiled as she thought about how lucky she was to have a man who cared so much for her that he would be willing to postpone the biggest business deal he'd had in twenty years, to be there to support her. He knew it wasn't going to be an easy trip for her, but he also knew she could handle it. She was hard wired to juggle twenty things at once and thrived while she did so. Kallie appreciated the support, even if it was from another continent.

"Welcome to Portland Jetport, folks! The weather is a sunny eighty-four degrees in Maine this afternoon. Thank you for flying with us and please enjoy your stay in Maine!" bellowed throughout the plane.

This was it. There was no turning back now. She was about a three- and half-hour drive from Somerfield, which meant that she was about three and a half hours from the worst people she had ever known in her life.

Fighting the nausea nerves as she exited the plane, she took a deep breath of fresh Maine air and said, "Here we go, girl. Hold on to the seat of your pants, it's going to be a hell of a ride. Getting out of here in one piece will take nothing less than a miracle."

She rented a car at the airport and headed North on I-95. There was no turning back now.

CHAPTER THREE

Driving North on Interstate 95, Kallie noticed that there seemed to be significantly more vehicles entering the state than were leaving in the southbound lane. As heavy as traffic was, in no way did it compare to the traffic flow in Virginia. Eventually, the rows of motels and car dealerships began to thin out giving way to not much of anything but lush, green pine and fir trees. Just a few miles further the traffic had all but disappeared until she was mostly alone on the highway. A soft evening light lay across the steep embankments on either side of the road.

Every now and again she passed a deer grazing on the grassy knolls. It always amazed her how they could go about their business of eating grass, with so many cars whizzing by and not seem to notice at all.

After a couple of hours any sign of buildings had disappeared as well. There was nothing ahead of her but blacktop and trees. The freshly paved highway rolled out like a long black and yellow ribbon. Except for a logging truck that passed every now and again, there wasn't much to look at. She had forgotten how desolate the long stretches of highway could be in that section of the state. Her mind began to wander, and an old but familiar fear and dread began to creep up until it smacked her square in the chest. The gnawing in her gut that she had felt most of the day was back also. Stronger than ever. There was an aching in her chest that she hadn't felt in an long time and hadn't missed at all. She knew the sick feelings coming over her came from a dark, uncomfortable place that she had somehow managed to stuff into the hidden recesses of her soul so very long ago.

Her hands began to shake, and she gripped the steering

wheel to steady them. One side of her brain kept nudging her to remember something. Something she had chosen to forget long ago. Whatever it was, she couldn't quite wrap her mind around it just yet but was painfully aware that it was there just in the shadows of her brain. There was a part of her that knew some skeletons should never be resurrected and she quickly tried to think of something else. It was no use. She was beginning to feel like it was no longer her choice to make. What the hell was happening to her? She fought to keep her eyes that had started to water with hot, burning tears, on the road.

Images of her mother coming toward her, hitting her as she tried to protect her face with her hands. Memories of her father hauling off and smacking her beside the head. Horrible, painful cries from her sisters. They were all there. The memories spiraled faster and faster through her mind until she couldn't fight back the flood gushing from her eyes. As the tears fell, she could barely see the road. She clicked the turn signal and pulled into the breakdown lane. She had to pull herself together. She had no idea what was going on inside of her, but she felt like she was losing her mind.

As a car flew by at breakneck speed jumping the daylights out of her, she thought of Cam and how she wished he were there with her. He was the strongest, most reassuring, supportive man she had ever known. What she wouldn't have given to have him in the car with her at that moment. That wasn't an option, and she knew it. It was important that he be exactly where he was for the time being. She could do this. She was a strong woman who had lived through so much worse. She wasn't going to let the ghosts of her childhood memories get the best of her. Besides, they were memories, not reality. They couldn't hurt her now. Could they?

Cradling the steering wheel, she bawled aloud. She saw Connie's face laughing at her. Mocking her, telling her what a failure she was over and over. Like a record stuck in the same groove. The old, much too familiar tunes, spinning in her head. "Useless, little bitch who will end up turning tricks on some street corner and have six kids before ya ever get to high school." and "Ms. Hoity Toity who thinks her shit don't stink but can't see she ain't nothing but trash!" played at warp speed, louder and louder. What was going on? Was she losing her mind? How was she going to get that cork back in the genie bottle now that it had popped off on its own?

She thought she had erased those monstrous, degrading tirades from that woman, a long time ago. Apparently, she had been very wrong about that.

"Living through it once was enough! I can't go through it again! I just can't!" came from somewhere deep in her throat. At first, she wondered where the sounds had come from. Was that *her* voice? That angry, vicious, determined sound had come from her?

Creating Kallie Douglas had not been easy. She had worked so extremely hard to kill off Kahlua Jansen. And suddenly there she was. The terrified, little girl was back. At that moment, she felt like time had stood still for the past thirty years or so. She almost felt like she had never left the sad dysfunctional hell hole at all. Everything she had worked so hard for…the self- respect, the confidence and most of all, the peace of mind, were quickly disappearing before her very eyes.

She felt unsure of everything she had previously known to be true. Everything that she took for granted just a few hours earlier, was leaving her. Panic took over her entire body and she felt like she was covered from head to toe with an icy overcoat. The chills and confusion made every thought of home and her life outside of Somerfield disappear. "My God, Connie was right! What right *do* I have to think I could ever be anything but that ragged, ignorant fleabag of a child? Who am I trying to kid? Hiding beneath the clothes, the cars, the trips, the make -up, the money, is that same screwed up little girl. I am always going to be Kahlua Jansen! Oh God! I *am* nothing but the "white trash" she prophesied me to be!" From somewhere deep within her, she felt her heart shatter into a million pieces as she struggled to breathe.

Suddenly it all had become so clear as though she had walked out of a dark room and into a too well-lit room. Who *was* she trying to kid? Underneath her storybook life was that same girl who was never as good as the other kids. She was still that child who was never dressed as nice other kids. Still the girl that was never as pretty as the other girls, and certainly never as shiny and clean. She was the kid left out of everything. The last one picked for games. The last one anyone wanted to know. In her head, she heard the words, so painfully loud and clear, "You can run girl, but you will never run far enough to lose me!"

She felt like the bottom had dropped out of her entire life in a matter of hours. Unable to contain any sort of emotion was not like Kallie. The out of control crying and yelling was not her either. Not usually. She howled like a newborn baby while tears rolled down her face. Her mother's voice continued to taunt her, "Happiness is for good folks and you ain't good Kahlua! Just you remember that girl!"

Screaming she cried aloud, "I hate you, Connie! I hate you so much! I don't know why you never loved me! How could you want such terrible things for me? A mother is supposed to love her child! Why didn't you love me? What did I ever do to you to deserve your hatred?"

She couldn't stop the voices and she couldn't stop the tears. No matter how badly she wanted to. She didn't want the memories! She didn't want to relive that hell all over again! She couldn't! She desperately wanted her life with Connie to have been nothing more than a bad dream that she could wake up from and make it not real. But it didn't matter what she wanted. She was speeding head on into a dark twilight zone and there seemed to be no way to put on the brakes.

17

A tap on the car window snapped her back to reality as it jumped the bejeezus out of her. Kallie strained to see through her blurred vision. When she did, she looked up to see a Maine State Trooper standing beside the car. She heard him ask if she was okay, but his voice seemed like it was coming from the far end of a long dark tunnel. She tried to speak but only soft whimpers escaped her throat. A deluge of tears broke free as she tried. Kallie could not stop crying long enough to tell him that she was okay. She wanted to but she couldn't. The truth was, she *wasn't* okay, and she was quite sure he could see that for himself.

She had difficulty catching her breath and could feel her weighted chest heaving as her lungs gasped for air. She felt her head slowly drooping forward as it came to rest against the steering wheel as the car horn blared into the air. Everything seemed to be moving in slow motion.

A wave of cool air hit the back of her neck as the officer opened the driver's door. He gently leaned her body against the back of the seat pulling her free of the horn. Kallie attempted once again to speak. Nothing but undecipherable garble came out of her mouth. Somehow, the officer managed to get the gist of what she was trying to say.

He spoke in a kind and soothing tone. "It's all right Ma'am. You're okay. You take your time and I'll stay right here with you" His voice was calm and reassuring. He asked if she knew where she was. Kallie shook her head. The truth was, at that very moment, she had no idea where she was aside the fact that she was driving north on I-95 in the state of Maine.

"Do you think you can pull yourself together and follow me just up the highway to the next exit? It's not safe for you to stay here on the side of the highway. These cars go by here pretty fast and some honestly don't pay attention to stopped vehicles."

Kallie nodded in agreement. "Just off the next exit there's a little diner that's open twenty- four hours. If you feel up to it, you can follow me there." he offered.

She squeaked out a feint "Okay."

As the Trooper walked back to the dark blue SUV parked directly behind her, Kallie took a deep sigh and reached for the rear-view mirror. "Oh, good Lord! I look like a freaking crazy person!" she whispered. She didn't know where all these emotions had come from, but she did know she was not okay with the out of control, insanity that she was experiencing. Driving up the interstate admiring the clouds one minute and a crazy basket case the next. She wasn't even in Somerfield yet and she was already a blubbering lunatic.

She reached for the handkerchief from her bag. A beautiful white silk monogrammed with KDD. One from the set of three that had been a gift years ago from Cam. One night, during their honeymoon, he had gone out for a business meeting and returned with them. He had commissioned a fine linen weaver in Switzerland to make them for Kallie and monogram them as well. KDD, that's who she was, dammit! Kallie Douglas! To hell with the nightmarish memories and crazy thoughts! She was NOT that person anymore! No matter how badly her mother had tried to screw her life up, she had failed.

She wiped the thick, black smudges that now stained her cheeks. Puffy, red blotches dotted her swollen eyes. She was a mess. Pulling out of the breakdown lane and onto the highway, Kallie thought, "That will be the *last* time I shed a tear for you Connie. The *last* time!"

The trooper led her to the diner and then took off quickly. Kallie figured he must have gotten another call. The building was small but had a cozy feel to it. A large sign on the red metal roof read, "Al's I-95 Dinr". The light behind the letter "e" had burned out. Regardless, the place seemed clean and well kept. Kallie didn't remember the last time she had been to a diner. In college most likely. There had been an old train car diner on the south side of town in Mt. Vernon that she and Cam frequented often. After a long night of studying, they would wander over to the rail car for breakfast. The place wasn't much to look at but the food they served was incredible. Fresh homemade cooking wasn't something the college kids enjoyed often unless they visited the Rail Car. She smiled as she remembered the countless nights the two of them spent at that diner. Cam would love this place. He had a soft spot for "greasy spoon" places to eat. Not that they'd had time to visit any in Lord knows how long. Dinner together was about a once-a-week event at their house, if they were lucky. Two workaholics do not make great chefs.

Inside the entrance a sign on a portable post instructed customers to seat themselves. Kallie quickly glanced around the room, chose a booth, and sat down. A long lunch counter located across from the door ran the entire length of the diner. Two men, who she assumed were the drivers of the two big rigs in the parking lot, sat at the counter on chrome stools with red vinyl seats. Every now and then, one of them would hysterically laugh aloud at something he'd seen on the television above the cash register. The quaintness of the interior also reminded her of the drug store in Somerfield that she had been to as a child. Murray's Drug Store used to have an old- fashioned soda fountain and a similar counter. She recalled how badly she wished she had enough money to buy a soda from that fountain. Sadly, she never did.

On the gray speckled Formica tabletop sat a miniature jukebox. Customers could insert a quarter and choose a song for the booth. It appeared to be an original, rather than a replicated version as it had its fair share of wear and tear. Looking around the room, Kallie guessed that the interior hadn't been updated in a long time, if ever. She decided it was part of what added to the charm of the place. The well-worn black and white checkered floor tiles were a testament to the foot traffic through the years.

A server wearing a pastel pink dress and a white apron across her front greeted her, "What can I get for you today?"

Kallie looked up at the fresh-faced young girl. "I think I'll have a cup of regular, no make that super strong coffee, if you have any of that?"

The young girl laughed. "Well, you've come to the right place. I've got half a pot left over from breakfast today. Last time I looked at it had a syrupy texture to it. That strong enough?"

Kallie grinned. "Sounds like just what I need!"

"Coming right up."

She noticed how young her server seemed to be. Was she even old enough to be working? She wouldn't have guessed her to be any older than a junior high school student. The older Kallie grew, she realized it was getting more difficult to guess people's ages with any sort of accuracy. It seemed to her that people looked younger and younger all the time. She smiled at the thought because she knew it was she who was getting older and young people just seemed to look younger and younger.

When the young woman returned with the coffee, Kallie asked for change for a twenty-dollar bill. She had spotted an old-fashioned cigarette machine on the way in and had every intention of dropping quarters in for a pack of smokes, no matter how stale they may be. The packs had could have been in the machine for twenty years and she didn't care. She pulled the knob and heard a pack of cigarettes drop into the opening.

As she took a drag from a very stale cigarette, a sense of calm slowly crept down her spine. The bundled- up ball of nerves in her stomach was beginning to unwind, just a little. As she sipped the thick, barely warm coffee, the thought of turning the rental car around and heading straight back to Portland popped into her head. She could take a flight back to Virginia and be back home by morning. She wanted to; she really did. Her brain wanted her to for its own self-preservation. Her heart was telling a different story.

The more she thought about it, the more she realized that the memories she had shoved to the back of the line for so long, would follow her there too. It sure felt to her that the universe was telling her it was time to deal with some things she had hoped to never face again.

She knew she would no longer be able to outrun the past. She had been fortunate enough, for a long time, to have the luxury of pretending. Now, there could be no turning back. As tempting as it was to leave, she knew it didn't matter where she went. It was time to pay the piper.

CHAPTER FOUR

After the day she'd had, it didn't take much to convince herself that she should find a hotel and stay put for the night. Driving any further than she absolutely needed was a bad idea in her current state and she knew it. Hopefully, a good night's sleep would clear the cobwebs. She headed for the pay phone in the corner and noticed the hanging chain where a phone book used to be. So much for the good ole yellow pages. She would ask for directions to the nearest hotel when the server came by again. Attorney Miller would wait until she got there so there was no sense in pushing herself. She was certain she could have fallen asleep on a rock at that point. Every ounce of energy seemed to have been drained from her body. Her puffy eyelids felt like they were held open by toothpicks or rather she wished she had some to keep them open.

Reading the local ads printed on the paper place mat, Kallie struggled to stay awake. A man's voice startled her. "Well, hello there! I must say you look a bit better than the last time I saw you!"

She looked up to see the trooper she had encountered earlier. He was a tall man with broad shoulders and a genuine smile. Even in the state of mind she was in, she couldn't help but notice how well he filled out the t-shirt he was wearing. Well defined, rugged arms protruded from the sleeves. His dark hair cut short and neat. He had very unusual brown eyes that Kallie noticed right away. They weren't a shade she often saw. Rather than deep brown, they were more of a creamy milk chocolate.

She paused a moment before speaking. She thought about telling him that she was fine, that she'd never felt better. She didn't bother. She knew the look on her face would tell a different story anyhow. She forced a half-hearted smile, "Well, to be honest, I've been better. I'll be okay though. I'd like to thank you officer...?" she asked searching for the proper name to address him by.

"Officer Wentworth. But I'm off duty now. Please call me Adam."

"Thank you so much, Officer Went...I mean, Adam, for your help today. And I promise I won't drive distracted again."

He grinned, "Well, I'm glad to hear that! I'm off duty for the night. One of my fellow officers may not be so understanding. Typically, we kind of frown on using the breakdown lane of the interstate as a place to apply make- up." As he teased, Kallie noticed the deep dimples on either side of his mouth and the deep chiseled cleft in the center of his chin.

"What? I suppose next you're going to tell me that the breakdown lane on the highway isn't the designated place to have a *mental* breakdown, either?"

Officer Wentworth smiled and laughed aloud. Kallie reassured him that she was done with interstate driving for the night. "I was planning to ask for directions to a hotel. I think I've been behind the wheel enough today. You probably know about everyone around here? Would you know of a place?"

"Well, I don't know *everyone*, but I do know of a place you can stop for the night. We're only a couple of miles from a nice bed and breakfast if you're interested in that type of lodging?" Kallie nodded and he continued, "A real nice couple own the place. The lady of the house was once a well- known chef in New York City before they retired to Maine. Amazing cook that woman is!"

Kallie agreed that it sounded perfect. A comfortable bed, a good night sleep, and a nice breakfast before hitting the road again was exactly what she needed. As he gave directions, he casually scooted into the booth without waiting for an invitation. He sat opposite her and quickly began sketching directions on a napkin he had grabbed from the table dispenser.

Kallie was glad for the company, even from a stranger. She tried to follow along as he spoke, but she wasn't really paying attention to the sketch. Her mind was wandering to distant places in her memory and then fading away into nothingness. Her head felt like it was hollow, and every sound made an echo. She couldn't remember a time when she felt so completely exhausted.

When she tuned back into the moment, Officer Wentworth had finished with the makeshift map he had drawn. He slid the napkin toward her. "Ma'am? Are you sure you're, okay?" he asked.

"I'm so sorry! My mind was somewhere else, I guess. "

"I see that. Have you eaten yet?"

No, I haven't. Just a couple cups of coffee but that's really all I need at the moment anyway."

"Just coffee? That's not good! Besides, I'm betting dollars to donuts that what you're calling coffee is leftover from morning. Al's not one for throwing out coffee. Says it gets better as the day goes on. Although, I don't believe anyone around here thinks that except Al. Now the food is another thing. Since you're already here, you should try that. I'll vouch for his food, but never his coffee."

She smiled. "I'm with Al. Tonight, this "mud" is exactly what I was looking for! I hadn't thought about eating, to be honest."

"Truthfully, I tend to eat here more often than I'd like to admit. Sometimes it's just easier than cooking for myself after I get off my shift. My wife also works nights quite often and eating alone gets old. The fact that it's right on my way home doesn't make it easy to drive past either."

"Oh, I see! That's why you were able to recommend this place to me. You didn't mention the cook is your personal chef!"

she teased.

"Well, there's that and you were already close by." He looked around as he spoke, "This place is small and not much to look at, but I tell you, they serve the best food in town. Sure, you don't want to try something from the menu? I think I'm up for a big ole greasy burger and fries."

As he told her about his favorites on the menu, it occurred to Kallie that she couldn't remember the last time she had sat down to dinner, one on one, with anyone but Cameron. Not that she had an opportunity to dine with him often either. Yet here she was, fresh off a mental blow out, sitting across from an incredibly handsome man. Adam convinced her to try the burger and fries platter. After they ordered, they sat in the booth talking as though they had known one other for years. Somehow, he didn't feel like a stranger at all. There was a familiarity about him that felt comfortable.

In no time at all, the server returned with their meals. "I challenge you to tell me where you've had a better burger, once you try this one!" he grinned and extended his hand across the table.

"Deal!" she shook his hand. "By the way, my name is Kallie, Kallie Douglas"

"Well, it's very nice to meet you, Kallie Douglas."

Although she hadn't felt hungry earlier, suddenly the large platter of French fries and the burger complete with cheese, tomatoes, and lettuce and pickles made her reconsider. She felt like she could eat the entire tray of food.

They were silent as they devoured the meal. "Well, Adam, you were certainly right about the food here. I didn't even think I was hungry, but I guess I must have been. I made short order of the burger and just about all of that heaping pile of fries!"

He smirked, "And? The burger? Best you've ever had?"

She conceded, "Oh most definitely THE best I've had any-where. Ever!"

He laughed and slapped the table. "Well, I guess it's a good thing I stopped in on my way home then. If not, you probably would have starved before morning!"

Kallie laughed. "Yes, thank goodness! I'm certain I wouldn't have made it through the night otherwise! Seriously though, I don't remember the last time a burger and fries tasted so good! Definitely hit the spot!"

He shifted in his seat, "Best food in Maine! Maybe even all New England! But I may be a little biased on that since they make so many of my meals for me and all. "

The server brought a carafe of coffee and left it with them. "This here's the fresh stuff. Just don't tell Al." She winked and walked away.

So, what brings you to Maine Kallie Douglas? Work? Family? Vacation?" he asked. Before giving her an opportunity to an-swer he added, "I'm sorry. That's none of my business! A haz-ard of the job I suppose."

She shook her head, "No. I don't mind at all. I used to live in Maine, once upon a time."

"No kidding?!"

"It was a long time ago though. Seems like a lifetime ago really."

"So, what are your plans for your stay in Maine?"

"I'm on my way to Somerfield. Well, right next door to Brad-ford, actually."

"Hmm. Neither one is exactly known for its tourist attrac-tions."

She shook her head and smiled, "No. I guess not. Unfortu-nately, a good friend of mine recently passed away. She was from

Bradford."

She could see his face begin to flush as he looked down into his coffee cup. It was obvious that he felt terrible for prying once he realized she was here for a funeral. "Oh. I'm so sorry, Ms. Douglas. I really need to learn to mind my own business. As I said, it comes with the job. I'm sorry for being nosey. I really am."

"First of all, please call me Kallie. Secondly, don't feel bad about a thing! You had no way of knowing. Trust me, I wish with all my heart, that I wasn't here for that reason. I'd much rather be staying in Bar Harbor enjoying the ocean view. But it is what it is. The service is for the woman who took care of me when I was young. She left her estate to me, and there's a bunch of things to deal with regarding that."

It felt odd to her to be talking about Maddie and that she had grown up in Maine. That part of her life had been gone a long time ago. To get on with her life and make something of herself that she could be proud of, she'd put the memories of Maine on the back burner. Until Maddie passed away, she'd had no intention of moving them to the front burner. Ever.

"Mrs. Douglas? Sorry, Kallie? Have I said something to upset you? You look like you've seen a ghost! You're as white as a sheet! If I did, I'm sorry. Please accept my apology, again, if I was rude or intrusive."

She looked across the table toward the calm and soothing voice, "Oh my goodness, No! You don't have anything to apologize for! I guess I'm just exhausted. It's been a crazy, weird, extremely long day." she explained.

"Understandable! Are you comfortable with the directions I gave you to the Bed & Breakfast?"

She shrugged her shoulders as if to say, "Not so much." The truth was, she hadn't heard much of anything he'd said regarding directions. Kallie stared at the scribbles drawn on the napkin. "So, I take a right at the next set of traffic lights, and then a sharp left or was that a left and then a right?" She tried to sound like she had some idea as to where she was going, though she had not the slightest.

He laughed. "Well, not exactly. If you go *that* far, you've gone *too* far. Why don't you just follow me, and I'll show you where it is?"

"No, I can't ask you to do that. You've done so much for me already! I'll find it…eventually, I'm sure."

He dismissed her refusal with the wave of a hand. "Oh, I haven't done anything. Certainly, nothing I minded doing. Seriously, follow me and I'll get you there. I'd feel better knowing you aren't wandering around in the dark trying to find the place." He slapped his hand lightly on the table after he spoke as if to emphasize that he would not take "no" for an answer.

Truth be known, she was grateful that he pushed the issue. She was losing steam by the minute and looking forward to sleep. It would take much more of a coherent mind to follow directions and she knew she just wasn't capable of at that point. Kallie gladly accepted his offer. "Are you sure you don't mind?"

"It's no trouble at all. Just a hop, skip and jump from where I live anyway."

Adam scooted out of the booth as Kallie did the same. Standing beside him, she suddenly felt small. At 5'5," he towered above her. She guessed he had to be at least six foot four." She hadn't realized earlier exactly how tall and sturdy he was. He led the way to the register and insisted that he pay for her meal as well.

An old- fashioned cash register, which had to have been a hundred years old, chimed each time the drawer opened. Made of brass and carved with swirled designs on the exterior, Kallie thought it was too beautiful to be in use. The small diner certainly had a warm and homey feel. Their server had been very attentive, and she appreciated the service and sense of humor she had shown them. As Adam paid for the meals, Kallie quietly returned to the booth and tucked a crisp fifty-dollar bill beneath her coffee cup.

She followed Adam to the bed and breakfast, which as it turned out, was a good thing he had offered to lead the way. She was certain she wouldn't have found it without him. As she drove, it occurred to her that she had genuinely enjoyed his company. It seemed like forever since she had enjoyed dinner with someone who didn't know who she was. For the first time in a long time, she had been able to be herself. That didn't happen often in her world. Cameron had made a reputation for himself around D.C. as a man who could get things done for people. And she was right there alongside him as someone who people looked up to for her ability to make things happen. It was unusual to find people in D.C. who didn't know either one or both of power couple. Officer Wentworth was different. He hadn't wanted anything from her but her company. In all actuality, he had been the one doing all the giving. Her evening had been one she wasn't accustomed to, but she had genuinely enjoyed herself.

Kallie pulled into a circular drive and parked in front of a wooden hand carved sign that read "Office." Adam parked just ahead of her then got out of his vehicle and offered to help her with her luggage. "Thank you so much for everything you did today. I really appreciate you going out of your way when you didn't have to. I'm all set with the luggage. I just have the one bag but thank you for offering."

Jiggling his keys in his hand he said, "You are most welcome. It was my pleasure, and I was glad to do it. I appreciate your sharing a meal with me. It's been nice to meet you, Ms. Kallie Douglas. Would you mind if I gave you my card in case you need anything while you're here in Maine?" He didn't wait for her to answer as he handed her a business card with his cell phone number and his home number written on the back. "If you need anything, please don't hesitate to call!"

Kallie couldn't help but notice the gentle, honest aura about him. Her intuition told her that he was a man who meant what he said and said what he meant. Cameron had that same quality about him, and she admired that.

Walking toward his Jeep Cherokee, he looked back and said, "You have a wonderful night and a safe trip."

She smiled back at him and walked into the office. A lovely elderly woman showed her to her room that was small but immaculately kept. Decorated in lodge decor with wildlife themed knick- knacks throughout. Paintings of black bears and white-tailed deer adorned the walls. In front of the picture window sat a small table and two chairs crafted from pine logs. A matching queen-sized bed stood against the back wall. A hand-made quilt in green and soft pink colors lay across the bed. Kallie was pleased to find the room inviting and comfortable. She couldn't wait to climb into the cozy bed.

***

Sitting on the edge of the bed, she wondered how it could be morning already. She realized she was still in yesterday's clothes. She'd meant to have a hot shower and change into her comfy pajamas but that never happened. She had been more exhausted than she realized. She fell back into the center of the bed, not wanting to get up yet. It was so comfortable. She could have laid there all day. But she knew that wasn't an option.

She reluctantly dragged herself into the shower. After she had thrown on a comfortable pair of jeans and a t-shirt, she went downstairs. At the foot of the stairs, a sign read, "Breakfast in the Dining Area" with an arrow pointing the way. She didn't know what they were cooking, but her stomach reacted to the incredible smells with a deep growl as she followed her nose to the dining room.

Adam had been right once again. The homemade breakfast was delicious. She had popovers, straight from the oven and dripping with freshly churned butter and Maine wild blueberry jam. After that she had a mushroom omelet made with eggs collected just that morning.

When she could eat not another bite, she stopped by the office to speak to the owners, Doris, and Russell James. They were exactly the kind of people who should be running a bed and breakfast. Both were kind, genuine, down to earth people who made it a point to invite her back anytime she wanted She took a brochure with her and promised to share with her friends back home.

On the road once again, she hoped it would be a better drive than the day before. She prayed for the ghosts of her past to stay away long enough for her to see to Maddie's affairs. She promised herself she would run as fast as she could straight out of the state after that.

"One step at a time, girl. You can do this. You *thought* it may not be easy and now you *know* it won't, but you got this!" she said aloud to herself in the car. It was time to pull up her big girl britches and do what needing doing.

Her first stop would be to Attorney Miller's office.

CHAPTER FIVE

Driving on the interstate, Kallie heard a song on the radio that she used to listen to back in high school. A smile crept across her face, and she found her fingers tapping on the steering wheel. Funny how a song can bring a person back to a place and time, in an instant. If only for a minute or two, it felt good to lose herself in old familiar beats blaring from the speakers."

Her mind drifted back to the days when she was learning to drive a car. Thankfully, Maddie had the patience of a saint. The main road through Somerfield, as well as Bradford, had been posted at twenty- five miles an hour back then. With a lead foot on the gas pedal, Kallie couldn't seem to get that old station wagon to "crawl" that slow. As the speedometer climbed, so did Maddie's tone of voice as she called out the speed limit. She could clearly recall the look on Maddie's face when Kallie told her, "It's so dumb to expect anyone to go that speed! Cars are not meant to go that slow!" She was sure she must have been responsible for more than a few gray hairs on Madeline's head.

Without the effort and infinite patience put in by Maddie, Kallie knew she never would have learned to drive at all. Connie made it perfectly clear to her children, even as young girls, that the only person who would ever be allowed to drive was going to be her. Making her daughters need to rely on her and only her for a ride was just another way for her to control them. There was no doubt in Kallie's mind that she still wouldn't know how to drive if she had never left that house.

She clearly remembered the day she passed her driver's exam and the look of sheer amazement on Maddie's face as she waved her license into the air like she'd just won the lottery. Truth be known, Maddie was probably surprised they gave her one at all. She taught Kallie to understand what a great gift she had been given with that license. She'd told her that it was a privilege, that if abused, could and would, be lost. Kallie would need to find a part-time job and pay half of the insurance on the station wagon she would be driving. She found a job after school at the only department store in town. That old green and yellow station wagon always got her to school, work and back home afterward.

Maddie never allowed her to purchase necessities with the money she earned, other than her share of the auto insurance. Kallie always had what she needed and then some. Maddie made sure of that. She said a young girl should have her own "crazy cash" to buy something for herself every now and then. She wanted Kallie to not only be responsible but to also treat herself for a job well done. She recalled how good it felt to have money for gifts that first Christmas after finding a job. Buying something special for Maddie with her own money had been the best part of that holiday. A gold-plated locket with Kallie's photograph inside had brought the woman to tears. It was that Christmas, that she'd called Kallie "daughter" for the first time. That day would forever be etched in her memory.

Her caregiver was always doing so much for Kallie and for everyone else in town, for that matter. She regularly took in work as a seamstress for extra money. People brought their torn clothing to her for mending, and she made them like new. Between her job in the kitchen at the elementary school cafeteria, and the odd sewing jobs, she was always busy. For graduation, Maddie had given her a check for twenty -five hundred dollars to take to college. Kallie knew how hard that money had come for Maddie. She had sewn for four years to save that much, and Kallie didn't feel right taking it as a gift. Maddie had insisted. She said she was proud that her "daughter" would be attending college and she was not going to let her go empty handed.

The local radio station played another four songs in a row

that she remembered word for word from her teenage years. Shocked that she could still remember the lyrics, she cranked the volume and sang along. The DJ came on to say, "Thanks for listening to 109.2, Maine's greatest oldies!"

"Oldies? What are you talking about Mr. DJ? That's MY music not oldies!" She growled at the radio. Thinking about it for a second, she realized that she *had* been out of high school for a long time now. How did that happen? She hadn't thought about high school in ages. There were plenty of good reasons why she hadn't. She always got along well with people at school but never had any true, real friendships. None that ever stood the test of time, anyway. All these years later, she realized that the ten-foot-thick wall she had constructed between herself and anyone who tried to become close to her may have been a good reason for the lack of friends.

In hindsight, Kallie knew that she was too afraid to have anyone get to know the "real" her. Knowing *her* meant that they may learn where she came from. She didn't want anyone to know what her early life had been like. She had been ashamed. Ashamed of who she had been born to. Ashamed of where she lived. Ashamed of everything associated with Connie Jansen. Though she had changed schools after going to live with Maddie, she was still reluctant to really open herself up to anyone. The fear of having anyone ever look at her with disgust as they did her mother, kept that wall strong and secure.

On the first day at her new school, she remembered telling everyone that she was an only child. She had told them all about the terrible accident that took her parents from her. Yes, both parents, sadly. Fortunately, she had her Aunt Maddie. The kids believed her and so that was the story she stuck to. What she hadn't realized as a child was that the fear of being compared to Connie had kept her in a prison of sorts. The emotional baggage she carried with her, even as a child was enough to destroy even the strongest of adults. Kallie learned quickly how to shut herself off from a lot of people. Most people. She excluded herself from good times and experiences growing up because of that fear.

Once she went off to college and was far from the Somerfield and Bradford areas, she felt free. For the first time in her life, she felt free of the stigma associated with Connie. She was free to reinvent herself and no one was the wiser. She had gone to a few parties for the first time in her life during the first year and realized all that she had missed. Not so much on the partying aspect. She wasn't what anyone would call a wild child. Drinking wasn't something she was ever going to make a habit out of. She saw in her parents what happened when drinking became something a person grew to enjoy a little too much. But she did come to realize that she had missed out on a lot of potential friendships. Not to mention the good old-fashioned fun that other kids her age had known. College was the first time she dared to take a chance and give others a real opportunity to know her. It was a time for Kallie to just be herself. Whoever she was going to become, it had been her time to figure that out.

A large green sign with reflective white letters told her she would be approaching the Somerfield exit in a few miles. She remembered thinking, when she left for college, that she would never see that sign again. She'd have bet her life on it.

Kallie thought of her life back in Virginia. It was ten a.m. on the second Tuesday of the month. That meant the woman's group she was part of would be having their monthly meeting. These were women she knew but she did not call them friends by any means.

Once a month they gathered to share gossip under the guise of the "The Women's Charity League of Vienna." Had she been home, she would have been present too. Not that she enjoyed the "gossip fest," because she despised it, but the group was one that donated an insane amount of money to the youth center as well as other charities that benefited children. The outreach center and homeless shelter were pleased to be recipients and truth be known, couldn't operate without the help. Each time they met, the over privileged women would catch up on the latest gossip, until they knew everyone's business. Never did they share their own dirty laundry, of course. Even though Kallie knew there was plenty of that to go around. She often wished she could skip the mindless chatter and simply collect the checks they wrote out after a few martinis. If not for the large donations they were making, she wasn't sure she could stand to see them all once a month just for fun. No. Without the donations, she *knew* she wouldn't choose to spend a single minute with any of them.

By now, they were no doubt wondering where she was and what could be keeping her. She never missed a meeting since she was the chairperson. The gossip wheels were no doubt churning while they tried to figure it out. If they knew where she was and why, they'd be burning up the phone lines across the state to share the dirt. She could hear them now.

"Evie? Joanna here. Listen, you are NOT going to believe what I'm about to tell you! Honestly, you are NOT! Well, I hardly believe it myself, but it's true. I assure you it's true! I heard from Buffy Charmsworth that every bit of it is one hundred percent true. How does she know? Well, she heard it from her hairdresser who heard it from the the Douglas' gardener, so I assure you, it's ALL true. Imagine...Mrs. Douglas....yes Kallie, wife of Camden Douglas.... well, I don't know how to say this without coming right out and saying it, Evie...Mrs. Douglas, come to find out, is well...she's common white trash from a dumpy shack in the middle of nowhere in Maine. Oh yes, Evie. It's true. Poor, poor Cam never could have known of her background! There is no way he would have married into a family like that...no... not coming from good parents such as his. He *couldn't* have known that she was plain white trash when he married her. Absolutely! She must have lied to him. Oh my gosh, to think he had no idea who she really is just was breaks my heart, I tell you!

Just *breaks* my heart!"

Undoubtedly, the conversations within the elite circles in town would go on that like for days. The gossip tree wouldn't stop growing until someone got to the bottom of something. It didn't have to be the truth. It rarely ever was but not one of them ever seemed to care about that. If it was something juicy for them to chew on, they were happy. As soon as one member was informed, another would be dialed up to fill them in and see what they knew. It would take a week of martinis and a trip or two to the south of France for the ole biddies to heal from the shock. Kallie could care less what they thought about her. She never really had. Her husband was another story altogether.

She never wanted to do anything that would jeopardize all that he had worked for at Douglas Enterprises. Cam had always known where she came from, and it never mattered to him. He was grateful that Maddie had taken her in when her own mother tossed her out like old garbage. Her childhood years were not something she shared with anyone but her husband. It was no one's business. She wasn't proud of her background, but she hadn't really been given a choice as to what family had been born into. The story she had created back in grade school was easier to repeat than explaining her morally bankrupt mother to her friends and acquaintances.

Sharp piercing pains began to sweep across her forehead. The repetitive pounding in her head was becoming unbearable. Every white line that flew past felt like she was looking through a kaleidoscope that was spinning at warp speed. Her heart began to pound so hard that she could almost feel it pounding against her shirt. The heavy, sinking feeling in her chest that she had experienced the day before was back. She didn't know what to make of it, but she didn't like it. Struggling to take a full, deep breath wasn't a feeling she was familiar with, nor did she like it one bit. She was a healthy woman of forty. What was going on? Was she having a panic attack? A heart attack? Whatever it was, needed to stop!

"This…. all of this…is YOUR fault, Connie. You are an evil, evil woman! Why were you ever allowed to be born into this world?" She heard the words, and she knew they were hers, but she felt like she was hearing them from a distance just as she had the day before. It sounded as though she was at one end of a long echoing hallway yelling into the nothingness. She kept hearing loud voices in her head. Voices of people arguing but was unable to make out the words they were saying. And then the cries for help were there again as well. A deep, heartbreaking sob, like one from a child who has bumped their head or skinned their knee grew louder and louder.

Thoughts and memories began to flood her mind. Little by little, Kallie began to remember things. As much as she did not want to, she started to have flashes of recognition. Suddenly, she knew the voices all too well. They were the cries she had heard in the darkness so many times. Some had been her own pleas for help. Some were her younger sisters, begging for help. The voices called out for someone, anyone to rescue them. Cold chills traveled from one end of her body to the other. The uncontrollable shaking had returned also. She felt her entire body quickly becoming uncontrollable.

"God! Please make this stop!" she cried, "I lived through this hell once already. Please don't make me do it again! I can't! I won't! Please, I beg you, please make it stop!"

But it wasn't stopping. The clouded confusion was only getting stronger. Time felt like it was standing still. It was as though it had stood still for the past twenty years, hiding just under the surface of her skin. As she drove, she felt the sting of the burning waterfall that covered her face. The more she tried to stop the stream of tears, the more they raged on.

The lines in the center of the highway were becoming increasingly difficult to see. Flashing white blurs whizzed by her. She had no idea if she was even in the right lane any longer. She hoped she hadn't passed the exit for Somerfield! If she had, she would have to go backtracking to make up for it. She tried to clear the blurriness to see where she was at that moment, but truly had no idea. She felt like she was in some spinning time warp. The tears, the dizziness, the memories were all on a loop, playing over and over. Reciting faster each time they played.

"Where the hell am I? Am I even in the right frigging lane? I shouldn't even be here! Oh God, what am I doing? I don't need this!" she yelled as she tried to wipe her eyes with her shirt sleeve and keep the other hand on the wheel.

The road, the fuzzy shapes of other cars on the road, the guardrails, all were becoming distorted and twisted. Kallie felt like she was blindfolded, flying down a bobsled run without brakes. It was as though all she could do was sit back and hold on for dear life as she flew down the highway at seventy miles an hour, blindly. She knew she shouldn't be behind the wheel in the state she was in, but the thought to pull over didn't seem to occur to her.

She continued to sob from somewhere deep. Maybe the absolute rock bottom of her heart, she wasn't sure. She cried for herself. She cried for the loss of Maddie. She cried for the baby sisters she had left behind. Years of penned up heartache had chosen that moment in time to rear its ugly head. She felt like the weight of the entire world had just dropped on her shoulders with a heavy crushing motion.

Why had she felt the need to return to this horrible place? Why did she have to be such an impulsive person? She told herself that if she had half an ounce of common sense, she would have realized from the beginning what a bad idea it had been. A very bad idea. "Who in their right mind voluntarily returns to the one place in the entire world that is the sole source of so much pain for them?" she shouted and answered herself, "People without any frigging common sense, that's who!"

She should be at home at her fund-raising meeting. At that

moment, she would rather be sitting across the table listening as the rich, over entitled whiners sipped their cocktails and gossiped. She knew she shouldn't have come to Maine. "What I should have done and what I did, well those are two very different things!" she burst out. She knew she'd always had a bad habit of doing things the hard way. The adventure north, she realized, was no exception.

Kallie couldn't shake the sense of impending doom that was slowly seeping through her chest. Reaching across the car to the passenger seat, she felt around for her handkerchief. Dammit! Had she put it in her bag? She swore she had seen it on the front seat earlier. She quickly glanced over to see that it had fallen to the floor. She reached for it, taking her eyes from the road for a split second.

What she hadn't realized, until it was too late, is that she had just approached the exit sign at about the same time. The car hit a cement traffic island and she lost all control. She felt herself soaring high. There was nothing beneath her but air as the vehicle rolled and rolled again in midair. And then she felt the bone shattering crash as the roof of the car landed against solid earth and everything went dark.

CHAPTER SIX

A call from the 911 dispatcher came across Officer Wentworth's scanner. A group of cars were blocking traffic in the northbound lane of I-95. When he arrived at the scene, a Canadian tour bus and six cars had stopped in the middle of the road. Within minutes, a large roadblock formed. An extremely excited older gentleman approached Adam, trying to tell him about an accident he'd just witnessed but he was talking so fast that he wasn't making any sense. Before long, an entire group of people gathered around the officer all trying to talk at once. Thankfully, another unit arrived and helped to lead the crowd and their vehicles to the side of the road. As soon as the vehicles were parked in the breakdown lane the officers started taking statements.

Finally, the elderly gentleman had caught his breath and was able to give details about a car that went "flying" over the embankment. The man and his wife were traveling behind the car as it left the road. As Officer Wentworth peered over the guardrail into the deep ravine below, he could see a vehicle resting on its roof. The entire area was eerily still. He saw absolutely no movement coming from the vehicle. Fortunately, there were no flames as sometimes happened when vehicles were involved in a crash of that magnitude.

Trying to keep his footing, he edged along the steep embankment toward the wreck. As he approached, he felt his heart drop clear to his feet. There in front of him, lying upside down on its roof, was a silver SUV that looked remarkably like the one Kallie Douglas had been driving the night before. "Please don't let it be her!" he prayed silently.

As he approached the vehicle, he saw what appeared to be

a lifeless arm lying on the ground sprawled out of the driver's window. As fast as he could, he ran across grassy terrain at the bottom of the gorge. Crouching beside the vehicle, he saw the last thing he wanted to see. Automobile crashes were never an easy thing to respond to, but it was even more difficult to see someone you knew involved in one. Unconscious in a pool of her own blood among a pile of twisted metal and broken glass, lay Kallie Douglas.

After quite some time and much effort, the Jaws of Life extracted her from what remained of the rental car. The process was lengthy and painstakingly slow due to the condition of the mangled metal. The location of the deep gorge didn't make access easy for the rescue team either. As the medics freed Kallie from the wreckage, a sigh of relief passed over the first responders when they managed to find a pulse. She was alive and Adam was grateful to hear it. He volunteered to escort the ambulance to Pineview Hospital once they had her loaded inside. It was a routine trip that he sadly knew all too well. This time was different though. He felt a connection to this woman. Less than twenty- four hours ago, he had shared a meal with her, shown her to the B&B and said goodnight. Now, he wasn't sure there would ever be another chance to talk to her. One of the paramedics told him that the chances of surviving a crash like that were slim. Adam knew they were right but hoped with all his heart that they were wrong.

Once at Pineview Hospital, Kallie was taken directly into the emergency room where she remained unconscious. Adam spoke to the physician on call, Dr. Roberts. who reported that Kallie would be prepped for surgery ASAP, as time was of the essence. If she were to stand any sort of chance at all, they would have to act immediately. He explained that large pieces of glass had become lodged in the center of her chest causing her to hemorrhage internally. She was also going to need at least one blood transfusion, if not more, depending how things went in the operating room. Dr. Roberts spoke frankly to Adam and told him that as much of the glass as possible needed to be removed from the chest cavity or she would die. It was that simple. She had already lost so much blood and had been unconscious for quite some time. Given those obstacles, he didn't dare to say one way or the other what her chances were of surviving. Further trauma would surely be evident once he was able to examine the patient closer but that was something the ER team expected in any accident. Get the big issues taken care of first and take it from there.

As the doctor passed the desk, Adam heard him tell a nurse to be sure the coffee was on because they were all in for a long night. He heard another nurse respond and he turned toward her. He knew that voice. In the craziness that had been his night, he had totally forgotten that his wife would be on duty by now. As he approached her, an O.R. nurse interrupted requesting an order from the blood bank for three pints of type O positive blood. Hopefully, the blood bank could get it to them ASAP. Adam let her know that he was a match and asked where he could donate on Kallie's behalf.

Amy smiled, "You are the most caring person I've ever known. You don't even know the patient and you're offering up your blood to her. I don't know how I got so lucky."

Even after five years together, she still knew how to make him blush. "Thank you love. I don't know how I got so lucky either. I do know the patient, by the way. Well, I don't *know* her, but I met her yesterday. She had pulled over in the breakdown lane out on the interstate and was having an emotional meltdown. I had her follow me to the diner so she could get her bearings before she attempted to travel any further."

"Oh, I didn't realize it was someone you knew."

"Like I said, I don't *know* her. I just met her last night. You were sleeping when I came in and were gone when I woke up. Otherwise, I would have mentioned it to you."

"Honey, that's fine. I just didn't realize it was someone you had so much as spoken to. That's all. Whatever the case, I think it's admirable that you didn't think twice before offering to donate blood. I think whether it was someone you had ever met or not, it wouldn't matter to you. You're that kind of person and that's part of the reason I love you so much." She looked up and down the hall to be sure they were alone and leaned in to place a kiss on his cheek.

They watched as the gurney carrying Kallie flew past them toward the operating room. He noticed the look on Amy's face when the patient passed her. She looked troubled, which wasn't like her. Adam had seen her treat the most horrific accident victims without so much as batting an eyelash. She was the kind of person who didn't hesitate. When there was work to do, she jumped right in and did what she could for her patients. This look was something he hadn't seen before and couldn't quite put his finger on what it was all about.

"Amy? You okay?"

Her furrowed forehead told him that she was deep in thought. "Amy? Hon? Are you okay?" he asked again.

"I'm okay. It's just that the patient on the gurney...that's the person you brought in from the accident?"

"It is. She's in pretty bad shape huh?"

"She sure does seem to be. I don't know for sure but for a second, she reminded me of someone. Silly, I guess. Half of her face covered in bandages and the other half ballooned up beyond much recognition. Been a long night, I guess. Anyway, I'm fine."

Adam agreed that it was hard to recognize much of the woman he had met the day before.

"What do you know about her, Adam? Family? Husband?" she asked with a pen in her hand ready to take down any relevant information for the chart.

"She said she lived in Virginia and used to live here in Maine a long time ago. Someone she used to know passed away and she was here to take care of the estate. She didn't mention a husband or any family by name though."

"That's too bad. I was hoping we could notify someone that she was here."

"The ambulance would have brought a purse or any personal items they may have removed from the vehicle. You may want to find out what came in with her. Maybe an emergency contact is listed in her things?"

"Good idea. I'll see what I can find out." She looked at her watch and then smiled at him. "Hey, aren't you off duty in about five minutes?"

The night had flown. Adam hadn't checked the time in hours. She was right, it was time for him to go home and get some sleep.

"One of those shifts! Time flew by today. I think it's time I head home and had me a shower and some sleep. If there's anything I can do to help, let me know. Oh! By the way, I do know that her name is Kallie Douglas. Jesus! I almost forgot that. Might come in handy to know that, huh?"

He scooted behind the desk after making sure no one was looking, and he gave her a tight squeeze and a kiss. "Get some sleep, babe. I'll see you tomorrow afternoon when I get up. Hey, it's your day off tomorrow, isn't it?" she smiled. "I don't have to be back here until seven p.m. It'll be nice to spend a little time together."

Adam flashed that smile that melted her every time. The strong cleft in his chin along with the boyish dimples still made her weak in the knees. After he left, Amy went to find the ambulance drivers who had brought Ms. Douglas in. Hopefully, with any luck, she would find a contact number to let someone know where she was.

Dr. Roberts was the on-call surgeon for the rest of the night and Amy knew that whatever could be done, would be done for the woman. He was a young, crackerjack surgeon who had come from California a short while back. Thankfully, he brought much knowledge of innovative procedures with him to their little hospital. She felt good about him being the one who would operate on the woman she had seen moments earlier. Whatever her issues were, there had been an awful lot of blood on the sheets that covered her. As she did with all her patients, she silently asked the Universe to watch over her and do what it could to help her. She still couldn't shake the feeling that she had earlier when the woman was wheeled past her. She looked familiar somehow, but Amy couldn't place where she would have known her from. But then again, Adam did say she was from Virginia, so probably she just looked like someone she had known at some point in time.

She finished making rounds to the ICU patients and went to the nurse's lounge for coffee. As soon as Ms. Douglas was out of surgery, she would be busy getting her settled into the open ICU room. It was now or never if she wanted a minute to enjoy her coffee. She had just finished adding creamer to her mug when Dr. Roberts came in. It had been about six hours since he had gone into the operating room.

"How did the surgery go? Is the patient ready to be wheeled down to the ICU?" she asked.

"Is there any left in the pot?" he asked looking at the coffee in her hand. She passed him the mug she had just made and turned to make another for herself.

"Thank you, Amy. I appreciate that. Her condition is still critical, no doubt about that. But I was able to remove the large shards of glass from her chest. If she can just get through the night, she may stand a decent chance. The bad news is that she hasn't been conscious since she came in. She's been in recovery for almost an hour now and should have woken from the anesthesia but has not."

Amy knew that typically patients woke from anesthesia within thirty minutes of the anesthesia reversal drug being administered. Dr. Roberts went on to say that he had seen a comparable situation one other time, but it wasn't a normal occurrence after surgery.

"The human body can do some crazy things, as you know. Sometimes after a trauma, like what this patient has been through, the body needs time to decompress. We'll have to see what happens over the next few days. Not much we can do for her now but keep her comfortable."

"I'll do my best. Speaking of which, I think she's ready for me. I'd best get her settled in her room. Go home, Doctor, and get some sleep the first chance you get. Been a long one for you."

Dr. Roberts was sitting on the sofa with his head tipped back toward the ceiling, looking like sleep might come at any minute. Amy shut the lights out on her way out and closed the door as she heard the first sound of snoring.

She met a nurse from the O.R. in the hall, returning Ms. Douglas from the recovery room. Amy wheeled the gurney into the room and went about hooking up the oxygen, monitors and fresh intravenous bags containing Morphine for pain, Heparin for the blood clotting issues as well as a Saline and Glucose solution. When she finished, she went about trying to find any personal items that may have come in with her. Fortunately, one of the ER nurses stuck her head into the room. She held a purse in the air apologized for not sending up the bag earlier. It had been a busy night for the ER as well. Besides the accident involving Kallie, they had been dealing with victims from a house fire, brought in as soon as Ms. Douglas was. Amy understood exactly how a crazy busy night in the ER could be. Pineview was a small hospital and oftentimes she worked in both the ER and the ICU and sometimes in the same shift.

Amy brought the bag into Kallie's room and began the uncomfortable job of going through her personal things. She never liked this part of her job. It seemed so wrong to be going through someone's personal things without their consent. A woman's purse contained important things that she kept close to her. Having a stranger go through them was not something people ever expect to happen.

She found a cellphone, but it was either locked with a pass code that she didn't know, or it was dead. Either way, the screen was dark and wouldn't turn on. That wasn't going to help her find someone to notify. At least not until the patient was conscious. She dug further into the purse and found a pamphlet for the local B&B. She rifled through the usual items often found in a patient's purse, lipstick, a key ring, hair ties. There also was a travel size bottle of Chanel No. 5, and a small leather-bound notebook with a snap closure on it. It appeared to be more of a diary than an address book. Still, as much as she hated to, she knew she had to open it and see if there was any information that would help her locate a relative.

Inside the book, there was a printout of an obituary and a photo of an elderly woman. She scanned the page but had no luck locating relative names. On the back of the photo was the name "Madeline Warren," but since she was deceased, that wasn't going to help her any.

Written on the first page of the notebook was the name of Attorney Miller. If all else failed, she could give him a call later in the day and see if he could provide any useful information. Other than that, the notebook was new and unused. She flipped through the pages to be sure and was surprised to see something written on the pages toward the back.

CHAPTER SEVEN

Amy woke to the warm summer breeze coming through the open window. The mesmerizing melody of the chickadees singing outside filled the room. She opened her eyes and didn't want to move. Instead, she laid in bed enjoying the moment. Adam knocked lightly and stuck his head in to see if she was awake.

"Good afternoon beautiful! Hope you slept well. Are you hungry?" he stepped into the room with a tray of food.

"Good morning, I mean afternoon. And just what do you have there? Did you dig out your chef hat again?" she teased.

"I did. I thought you might be hungry. I heard you come home this morning, later than usual. I know it must have been a long shift for you."

She moved over to make room for him to sit on the edge of the bed. "It was definitely a long night, and I am starving. Thank you so much honey. You are honestly the best!"

"Two pieces of French toast, one sausage, coffee and orange juice. It's all I could scrounge up for breakfast. We've both been working so much lately, taking extra shifts, that the grocery situation is a little slim. I'll stop a little later and stock up."

Amy shook her head as she smiled at him. What had she ever done in this world to deserve a man like him? "Thank you so much for breakfast, for loving me, and for being you."

She leaned forward to give him a kiss and then dove into the tray of food. She felt like she hadn't eaten in weeks although it had just been the day before. The hospital had been too busy for her to take a dinner break the night before and she felt famished.

"How was your patient last night? Did she wake up yet?"

"She hadn't when I left. Dr. Roberts said it happens sometimes but it's rare for someone to not wake up when there doesn't seem to be a medical reason behind it. He once had a patient in a coma like state sleep for a while, with absolutely no reason for it. He said sometimes the body responds weirdly to trauma. He thinks it should pass."

"Well, I'd trust him with my life. If that's what he thinks, I'd take his word for it. I hope you were able to find someone to notify on her behalf?"

"Unfortunately, no. I went through her purse but had no luck. She had a cellphone that is either locked with a password or the battery is dead, one or the other. Besides that, just the regular things that are in every woman's purse. I did find a notebook though."

"Oh? Anything useful in there?"

"Not really. But there was a half-finished letter written to a woman she had kept an obituary for. I probably shouldn't have read it and now I kind of wished I hadn't." she said in between bites.

"Oh? Why do you feel that way?"

"I don't know. It's just that in the letter, she talked about being homeless at ten years old and how the woman took her in and raised her as her own when her own mother couldn't. All night after that, I kept wondering what would make a ten-year-old child homeless? I mean, where were her parents?"

Adam cocked his head to the side as he thought. "Well, I don't know. I guess there could be lots of reasons. Depends on the situation, I guess. It's going to bug you now, isn't it? Knowing that she has no one with her right now?"

He knew her too well. She had big heart and never was particularly good at hiding it. He had seen her volunteer for extra shifts so her co-workers could stay at home with a sick child.

He had seen her work double shifts so a co-worker could go on a field trip with their child. She was always doing things to help other people and he knew that she was happiest when she was doing for others. Amy never asked or expected anything in return. That was part of the reason he loved her like he did. And the reason he tried to do little things like bring her breakfast after a long shift at work. It wasn't much, compared to what she did for him and everyone in her life, but she appreciated everything he did for her.

"I don't want it to but yes, I think it's going to be hard knowing that until she wakes up, there will be no one with her. Plus, when I read that letter, it made me think of all the times I prayed to God that I was a homeless orphan so I could have a different mother. I felt bad feeling that way when this poor girl really was in that boat."

Adam looked at the beautiful woman who had the kindest heart he'd ever known. All five feet of her, with her one-hundred-and-thirty-pound body, and dark chestnut hair, was an angel. His angel. She had come into his life and saved him from the workaholic he used to be. Never did he imagine he would have the love of someone as special as Amy. Every day he was thankful for her. Every day their relationship drew them closer.

"Don't feel bad about wishing that for yourself, sweetie. First, you were just a kid. Secondly, knowing your mother the way I unfortunately do, I don't blame you a bit for feeling that way. I'm quite sure anyone in your shoes would have wanted a different mother. No offense.

Amy laughed as she finished off the last piece of French toast. "No offense taken my love. You don't know the half of it."

"And it's probably a good thing I don't. Loving you the way I do; it kills me to think of what you must have gone through."

"Eh, it's okay. I made it out in one piece. Mostly. So back to the patient for a minute. I think when you start your shift tonight,

I'll just go by and poke my head in for a minute. You know, just to see how she's doing."

Adam moved the tray from the bed and sat it on the floor, smiling as he did so. "What? On your day off? You're going in to work? Why that just can't be!" he took her into his arms and kissed her face all over. He moved down to the ticklish spot on her neck and laughed as she squealed.

Amy begged him to stop and showed him the goosebumps on her arms. "See what you do to me!"

Adam raised his eyebrows. "Oh, I haven't even begun to show you what I can do to you. Looks like I have hours before I need to leave for work. You, young lady, are mine for the afternoon."

There was no place Amy wanted to be more than with this man she absolutely adored. Work could wait.

CHAPTER EIGHT

The privacy curtain was closed when Amy reached Kallie's room. She peeked through the opening to see the day nurse changing out the empty IV bags. "Hello Sheila, how's she doing?"

"Hey Amy! Aren't you off today?"

Amy rolled her eyes. "Yeah, but I just wanted to come see how Ms. Douglas was doing."

"Uh-huh so you're going to check on her and go home and enjoy your night off, right?" she grinned.

She had worked alongside Amy too long to believe that was true. Amy took a personal interest in all her patients. Sheila respected the hell out of her as a nurse and as a person. More than once, Amy had gone to bat for her. When her daughter had the chicken pox and couldn't go to school, it had been Amy that took over her shifts for her for two weeks. She was always helping wherever she could and Sheila, as well as the other nurses as Pineview appreciated and respected the person she was.

"Oh, I don't know. Maybe. So, has there been any progress since I left? Any conscious moments at all?"

"No, sadly none. I heard we have no relatives we can call?"

"No and that's bugging me to no end. I mean, it's bad enough to be in a car accident and it's worse when you have no one there to care if you ever wake up or not."

Sheila grinned. "Well, I'd say that's not entirely true. You *did* come in on your day off to check on her now, didn't you? Why do I think you'll be here every day off until you find a family member that can be here?"

"Sheila, you just know me too well, girl! I know. I know. I'm a sucker for a sad story, I guess." she moved a spare blanket from the reclining chair next to the bed and sat down. "I'll just hang out a bit if you don't mind. If I get in your way, just kick me."

"You're never in the way Amy. And somehow, I knew you may be around today. Okay, since you're here, I'll go tend to my other patients. Let me know if you need anything or if she wakes up." she patted her on the shoulder as she left the room.

Amy looked at Kallie's face. In just a few hours' time, the swollen bruised face was turning into more of a purple color with deep yellows mixed in. It must have been one hell of an accident. Adam said she went completely over the embankment and all the way down to the gully below. Amy knew it was a miracle that she was alive at all. She remembered that she forgot to ask Adam earlier at the house if Ms. Douglas had mentioned anything else when he spoke with her at the diner. Probably not or Adam would have mentioned it. Still, she'd call him and see if there was anything he may have put in his report that he had forgotten to tell her.

His phone only rang twice, and he answered. "Hey babe, you miss me already?"

Amy smiled. "Of course, I do love. I always miss you when we're not together. But I did call for another reason too. When you spoke with Ms. Douglas at the diner the other night, did she say anything that you may have forgotten to mention? I know you tend to write detailed reports and was hoping you had forgotten to mention something to me."

"Like?"

"I don't know. Something that we could use to find out more about her."

"Sorry love. I told you what I knew. She was going to Somerfield for a funeral service, or she was going to plan one, I think. Something about the house the elderly woman once lived in needing selling, I believe. Hmm let's see, I think that's about it.

She didn't really say a lot about herself. Though she didn't say so, I did feel that something other than the funeral service may have been nagging at her. The woman had this deep sadness about her, but I couldn't put my finger on what that was all about. Could have been the death of her friend and that was all. I really don't know. I wish I could tell you more."

"That's okay. We will just have to wait until she wakes up."

"Honey? Tell me you are home doing something enjoyable? Reading a book maybe? Or enjoying a nice long, relaxing hot bath?"

"Umm okay. I can tell you that if you'd like." she laughed.

"I knew it. As soon as I left you hightailed it for the hospital, didn't you?"

"Not as soon as you left. Maybe a few minutes after."

Adam was laughing now. He knew she would go back to Pineview for the evening. There was no way she was going to let that woman be alone should she wake up and not know where she was or what had happened.

After she hung up with Adam, Amy sat and wondered what this woman's story was. What kind of life had she come from in Virginia? Was there a someone special who would like to know where she was? What happened to send her into that gully? So many questions she wished she knew the answers to. She lifted Ms. Douglas' left hand and held it.

"Ms. Douglas, I don't know what your story is or who you are, really. But I want you to know that I won't let you be alone through this if I can help it. Until I can find your family or a husband or whoever it is that cares about you, I will continue to be here for you."

Amy wandered down the hall and entered the elevator bound for the cafeteria. There was a coffee machine on the ICU floor, as well as a coffee pot that ran twenty-four hours a day.

Neither was something she chose to have on her day off when she didn't need diesel fuel grade coffee coursing through her veins.

The partial letter in Ms. Douglas' notebook was still bothering her. She didn't know squat about this woman but the fact that she had been an orphan at such an early age made her sad. The letter had stirred feelings and thoughts of her own mother. A subject that she rarely thought about these days. And for good reason. Plenty of good reasons. She hadn't been exactly the kind of mother any child would want. She certainly had wished more than once for a different mother. Someone who cared. Someone who wasn't short sighted and selfish. As much as she prayed for a guardian angel to take her away from her mean and nasty mother, it hadn't happened. She never knew what it was like to be a child without a place to lay her head. Her home hadn't been much to speak of, but it was at least a roof over her head.

What Ms. Douglas must have had to deal with being alone and homeless as a little girl. When she thought about it all now, maybe her childhood wasn't that bad. She found herself feeling a little grateful, which was something she never once thought she could feel about it. Gratitude for her home and her mother was an absolute first for her! Regardless of the hell hole it was, she hadn't been alone. She'd had her siblings to help her get through the hard parts. The poor woman who lay unconscious in the hospital bed, had no one by the sounds, until the elderly woman took her in, anyway. Amy couldn't even imagine what she must have been through. She did know that she wasn't going to let her go through the current situation on her own.

Her cell beeped as she exited the elevator. It was a text from Adam offering to stop by and buy her a gourmet meal from the cafeteria. He was taking his dinner break in ten minutes and would meet her there if she were interested.

She texted him back. "Love to! I just rode the elevator down to the cafeteria. Will get coffee and wait."

She sat at a table in the back waiting for Adam. Her mind drifting back to her childhood. What would she have had to do, she wondered, to make her mother kick her to the curb at ten years old? She'd always felt her mother had no loyalty to anyone but herself, but she wondered if even *she* could have done that to one of her children. The more Amy thought about it, she realized if her mother could have, she would have. It sure would have been easier for her than having three mouths to feed when all she really wanted to do was stay drunk twenty-four hours a day. No, the more she thought about it, she decided even *her* mother wasn't screwed up enough to do something like that.

Adam arrived and halfway through his tray of macaroni and cheese, his phone went off. A car-moose accident at the furthest point north in the county. Not something he wanted to hear. It was always a long night when he had to make the three hour long drive that far north. If it had been a straight road all the way, that may have been different. But the road up there was nothing but one winding curve around a mountain after another. Deer and moose roamed the highway in the dark, so he always had to lower his speed to watch out for them. It was going to be a longer shift than he had anticipated, he could see that already.

"I'm sorry love but I have to go. You know how it is. I'm glad I got a minute to see your beautiful face tonight." he smiled.

"You, my dear, are quite the charmer. I'm glad I had a minute with you too. I think I'm going to go check on Ms. Douglas one more time before I head out. I've plenty of chores at the house I should be doing."

"Okay. Drive safe and I love you." he whispered into her ear as he stood to give her a kiss goodbye.

"YOU drive safe! Watch out for those critters up north!"

She watched him walk away in his navy-blue uniform and black polished boots. He was as handsome to her then as he had been five years ago. Every day of her life she felt the warmness in her heart and gratitude for him. She realized right off the bat after meeting him, that he wasn't like any other man she'd ever known. Right from the start, he had been more concerned with her wants and needs than his own. His loyalty and commitment to her was something she hadn't found in anyone else she had dated. Not that she'd had a lot of relationships before him. She hadn't.

She did have one long term relationship with a man who thought it was her duty as a woman to tend to his every desire and need in life. She stayed too long, and she knew it. She had been working her way through nursing school at the time and knew that one big hurdle at a time was all her mind could handle.

It didn't take long after she graduated and received her license and became an RN, for the relationship to dissolve. Not that it was ever a relationship. It was a one-way street designed around her doing whatever she had to do to make him happy. It hadn't started out that way, but it ended that way. Jared lured her in with kindness and sweetness. Once they made the decision to move in together, it all went south. He thought he had himself a house cleaner, a chef, and a lover any time he wanted.

Oh, and there was the fact that he believed that what was his …was his and what was hers …was also his. She was expected to hand over her paycheck to him each week and that was not up for discussion. He would pay whatever bills needed paying and then would give her a small allowance each week.

After the life she had come from with a controlling mother, it all seemed like it was what should be happening in a relationship. Amy hadn't ever had a happy couple parent role model to learn from. It was always her mother and her mother's boyfriends that she learned from. The drinking too much, arguing, throwing plates at one another's heads weren't the healthiest lessons to learn. But it was all she had. Her father had long taken off after she was born, and Amy had absolutely no memories of him. Her friends tried to tell her that Jared wasn't treating her like she should be. She had no idea how she was supposed to be treated by a man. Until the day she went to the bank to withdraw money out.

A co-worker and her family had lost everything they owned in a house fire. Donations were collected for the family to help them stay in a hotel while the insurance information was sorted out. Amy and the other nurses at Pineview were starting a collection and each pledged to donate one hundred dollars. When she went to her bank, she was informed that her account was in the red for two hundred dollars. She had no idea where her paychecks had been going each week, but she had trusted Jared to do what needed to be done for the household. He had been doing what was right for him and only him. That was the wakeup call she finally needed to get out. The next pay period, she was sitting in her new apartment.

Two years later, she and Adam met at the hospital while they were both on duty. He had come in regularly but before that night she had hardly ever talked to him unless it was about a patient. One evening he hadn't brought anyone into the ER and there had been no prisoners in the ICU, yet he was at the nurse's desk when she got on duty.

She hadn't been at work five minutes when he asked her if she was interested in getting a coffee from the cafeteria with him, on her next break. She didn't know what to think of him. She hadn't had a date, even for coffee, in two years since being on her own. She was sure it was because she purposely put out those "leave me alone, not interested" vibes. Adam hadn't gotten that message from her. He was interested and his timing couldn't have been better.

She had spent the previous two years working through things from childhood, from adulthood and everything in between. After the abusive relationship she had left, she worked hard to figure out what made her ever want to be with someone like Jared in the first place. She knew it was important to stay single until she learned whatever she needed to learn to stop attracting a partner who wasn't on the same page as herself. Two years of therapy had shown her things about herself that she had truly never known. She didn't have the luxury of a life where her mother told her she could be anything she wanted. She was never told that she was loved. No one ever praised her for a job well done; instead, there were always complaints of a job not done well enough. With therapy she learned to put herself first in a healthy way. She had figured out what she wanted in a relationship and what she would never, ever put up with again. She grew to understand that she was worthy of love, support, kindness, and respect. That was a particularly hard lesson get through her head. At that time, she was twenty-two years of age and had never understood that she *deserved* those things.

She felt like she was in a good place, emotionally by the time Adam asked her to have coffee. Then there was a second date to a local winter carnival put on by his state police troop. It seemed that after the second date, they were inseparable. Within a year of dating, Adam proposed and Amy, who once thought she would never know the love of a real-life knight and shining armor, had found exactly that.

Adam's parents had both passed away and Amy did not want her mother to be within a thousand feet of their wedding. They eloped and had her sister, Ginny, and his best friend, Brad with them as witnesses. It was a beautiful ceremony at the Castle in the Sky Grand Hotel in New Hampshire. They stayed for the week and hiked, swam, ate gourmet dinners some days and others had a packed lunch from the kitchen to take with them to explore. It was everything Amy had ever imagined and more. And there they were now coming up on their fifth wedding anniversary. There hadn't been a single day of arguing between them in those five years.

Adam made it easy to be happy in her marriage. He was always sending her flowers at work, unexpectedly, for no reason at all. No reason other than the fact that he absolutely loved her. He was always doing things to surprise her. Whether it was cleaning the entire house and doing all the laundry, so she didn't have to do it on a day off or cooking a meal for her after a long day at work, he was always doing something to show her how much he cared.

Amy did unexpected things for him too. On a day off she would make his favorite meal and surprise him with a nice dinner or order a case of his favorite IP from a brewery in New Hampshire. Whatever it was that each did, it always had what was best for the other in mind. She pinched herself sometimes just to see if it was real. It was. He was. They were.

As soon as the elevator doors opened, she could see the commotion around Ms. Douglas' room. She felt her heart drop to her feet. Something had happened while she was gone.

CHAPTER NINE

As much as she wanted to run directly into the room and find out what was going on, Amy stayed back and out of the way. She wasn't on duty and the last thing her co-workers needed was her to be underfoot asking a million questions. When the frenzy died down a bit, she would find out what was happening.

In the brief time she had stood against the wall across from the ICU, she had seen the phlebotomist come and go as well as the respiratory therapist. There were still two floor nurses and a CNA in the room. One by one the room emptied out except for the charge nurse, Susan Chambers. She and Amy had grown close through the many years of working together. She felt it was a suitable time to get in there and find out what had taken place while she was gone and prayed silently that it wasn't something bad.

Susan was pouring ice water into an adult sized sippy cup with a straw when she walked into the room. "Amy! I wondered where you had run off to. I didn't figure you'd gone too far."

"Adam and I were in the cafeteria downstairs until he got pulled away for an accident up north. When I got off the elevator, I saw the parade in and out of here and thought it best to keep out of the way. What happened, Susan?"

She looked at Ms. Douglas who was lying in the bed with her eyes closed just as she had left her an hour earlier. "Well, we had a little commotion with Ms. Douglas while you were out. Seems she decided to open her eyes when the custodian was in the room cleaning up. She was attempting to call out to someone named, "Maddie." By the time we got in here, she was asleep again. But hey, that's a good sign I'd say!"

Amy was relieved that it was not something terrible that had taken place. She breathed a sigh of relief. "That definitely is good news! And, with the ventilator removal earlier, who knows, she may wake up for good, anytime now."

"I wouldn't be surprised if that's the case. The poor woman has to be exhausted, both mentally and physically. When her mind's ready for her to deal with it, she'll wake up. I have no doubt."

Amy knew she was right. She couldn't imagine the trauma this poor woman had been through and somehow managed to come out the other side alive.

"If you don't mind and if I won't be in the way, I'd like to stay for a bit, Sue."

Susan laughed. "Of course, I don't mind and I kind of figured we'd see you around now and again until she woke up."

Susan gathered up the empty IV bags, the disposable gowns and used gloves and left Amy to sit with Mrs. Douglas. She pulled a chair closer to the bed as quietly as she could. She would text Adam while she was thinking of it and give him an update on the patient. She knew he was hoping for the best for this woman as well. She had just pushed "send" when she noticed the lifeless hand flinch a couple of times and then stop.

****

A hurricane force wind was blowing all around her. Kallie could see there was nowhere to run to. She would have to find shelter as much as she could in the rickety old barn. She dove behind a stack of hay bales as lightening lit up the barn and a clap of thunder cracked directly above her head. Looking around she could see that she wasn't alone. There were chickens, a cow and a few goats roaming around the barn as well. Were they as cold and scared as she was? They started running, each forming their own little circular path. Over and over, they ran gaining momentum and picking up speed as they ran in a big circle. A rusted antique farm tractor stood like a sentry in the center of the floor. Where was, she? She didn't own a barn. Or animals. Or a tractor.

Another round of thunder cracked just above her, and she tried to yell for help as the wind shattered the window high above her. Only there was no sound when she opened her mouth. Suddenly she could feel the hot breath on the back of her neck. Someone was behind her. Her heart raced faster, and her legs felt like rubber. She had to get out of there. But where could she go? She was sure to die if she went outside in the storm. An old, rusted horseshoe fell off the wall and landed beside her. She went to reach for it, but hers was not the hand to reach it first. She shook with fear as she tried to figure a way out and away from whoever or whatever was sharing the space in the dark with her.

It was then that she saw the woman. Was that Maddie standing at the barn door? What was she doing out there? She was sure to get struck by lightning! She needed to get away from that door! Kallie tried to yell out to her but once again, there was no sound. Somehow, she had to get to Maddie. She had to get to her before whoever sat behind her breathing heavy in the dark, got to her first. "Maddie! Run!" she screamed silently. Maddie didn't hear her. No one heard her.

"Ms. Douglas?" Amy whispered.

"Maddie? Is that you Maddie?"

Amy stood from the chair and leaned toward her. "My name is Amy. I'm a nurse here at Pineview Hospital, Ms. Douglas."

Kallie's eyes were completely open now. "Hospital? What?"

"Yes. You are at Pineview Hospital Ms. Douglas. Everything is going to be fine. You've got a great crew taking care of you here.

Her voice was raspy and dry. "I feel...I feel like I swallowed a cactus. My throat is killing me."

"Here, let me get you some water. You were on a respirator

for a while and that tends to leave the throat a little tender. That will go away in no time." she held the straw for the patient as she struggled to sip.

"What happened to me?" she asked.

"You were involved in an automobile accident, but Dr. Roberts fixed you right up. I'm going to let the nurse on duty know that you are awake okay. I'll be right back."

Kallie looked confused. "I thought you were the nurse?"

Amy gave her a warm smile. "Well, I'm *one* of the nurses who have been taking care of you but I'm not on duty today. I just came by to see how you were doing."

"That's so nice of you. What did you say your name was again?" she tried to force a feint smile as she spoke.

"My name is Amy. I'll be back in two shakes of a lamb's tail. You sit tight okay."

When Amy returned with Susan, Kallie was asleep again. "Well, she *was* awake. I'm sorry to drag you in only to have her be asleep again."

Susan dismissed her with the wave of her hand. "No worries, Amy. I'm glad to see she is starting to come around more. Maybe by morning, she will be completely back with us."

"I sure hope so. Okay, I feel better knowing she isn't in a coma. I think I'm going to head home and make a meal for Adam, for later when he's off duty. I'll be back tomorrow morning."

Susan laughed. "You don't have to do that you know. Days off are meant to be *off*. Besides, if I had me a man like Adam Wentworth, I'd be wanting to spend every available second at home with him." she winked as Amy's face blushed.

"We take our time when we can get it. With both of our weird schedules, sometimes it's dinner at midnight or breakfast at two p.m."

Susan understood how difficult it was to have a relationship with nursing hours, let alone a marriage. "You're lucky to have a man who understands your dedication and devotion, my dear friend. But then again, he's just as lucky. I know he's as dedicated to his job as you are to yours."

Amy agreed and said goodnight. She was looking forward to some quiet time with Adam when he got home later. She made a pan of lasagna, a garden salad with toasted French bread and happily joined her husband for a meal at 2 a.m.

****

The room was dimly lit when she opened her eyes. She could see from the window beside the bed that it was dark outside. How long had she slept? One minute she was talking to a nurse and the next she was out cold. She was still so tired. Her eyelids felt like they weighed a thousand pounds each. Had they given her something to make her groggy or was she just really that tired? She recalled the conversation with the nurse earlier. She was in a car accident? Is that what she had been told? She wasn't sure what was real at that point. It all felt like she was in a dream. She tried to lift her head from the pillow but a pain like she had never felt before went from one side of her head to the other. What the hell had happened to her?

"Okay. Not a dream. The feeling of a knife being driven into my head is real." she gasped.

She felt the nurse bell in her right hand where someone had taped it in place. She pushed the buzzer with her thumb and waited for someone to come. She needed something for the excruciating pain in her head. The blinding white light piercing her eyes with every blink was more than she could take.

Where was the nurse? Somebody had to hear the bell that

she was pushing incessantly at that point. Slowly she started to feel like she was on a ride at an amusement park. The room started moving around and around in circles and she felt warm all over. Her head didn't hurt anymore. Nothing hurt. The pain was gone as she enjoyed the ride in her mind.

CHAPTER TEN

The bright light streaming into the room shot through her head as she tried to wake from the groggy sleep. Without thinking, she threw back the covers and tried to sit up. It only took a second for her to realize that she was attached to tubes and wires and wasn't going anywhere. Not that she could have walked anyway. Though she didn't yet know it, her right leg was broken in two places. The surgeon had refused to operate until she healed for a few days. She'd been through extensive surgery just a short time ago.

She knew something was wrong with her leg because it hurt like hell. Frustrated, she lay back on the pillows and tried to remember how she ended up there in the first place. She remembered driving on the highway. She knew the turn had come up too quick. She remembered her eyes clouded with tears and the deep-seated feeling of desperation she was feeling at the time. And then she remembered flying over the embankment and the hard crashing force on her head as the vehicle landed upside down.

It had been those wretched memories that landed her in the hospital bed. The memories she fought for so many years to forget. "This is what happens when you let them come to light, Kallie. You knew that you damn fool. Why'd you have to come back here in the first place?" she whispered.

Maddie was why she was there, and she was the only person that could have brought to her back to Maine. There was no way she wouldn't come for Maddie's service. A service that she was supposed to arrange. How long had she been in this place anyway? She needed to go. She had things to do. Things that could not wait! Where did that nurse go? Someone needed to unhook her from the web of machines that surrounded her. She was getting out of that bed! She was not going to let Maddie down. Not this time.

As she followed the maze of tubes and wires with her eyes, she knew she wasn't going anywhere. Even if she wanted to, she was hooked to a web of wires and tubes and couldn't go anywhere. Finally, she heard a knock at the door. Great timing! Hopefully, it was the doctor coming to release her. If it wasn't, then she would send whoever it was to get the doctor who *could* release her from this place. She was getting out. One way or another she was leaving.

A woman's voice spoke softly. "Good morning. Are you awake?"

Kallie's impatient tone snapped, "I'm awake! Come in here and unhook me from this mess of tubes and wires. I have to go! I have somewhere I need to be!"

A vaguely familiar face peeked around the curtain. It was the nurse who had visited with her the night before. Good! She seemed nice enough. Maybe she could help her.

"How are you doing this morning?"

"I'm fine. I just need help unhooking these things. Can you help me? I really need to go. I am supposed to be somewhere!"

Amy smiled apologetically. "I'm sorry Ms. Douglas, but I can't do that. You can't go anywhere just yet. You had quite a crash recently. Dr. Roberts removed a lot of glass from your body, and you will need surgery on your leg at some point. How are you feeling besides anxious to leave?"

"I feel like I was run over by a truck. A big truck! How long have I been here?"

"Today is the fourth day you've been here, although I'm

sure it doesn't feel that way to you."

"Are you kidding me? Four days? Jesus! I was supposed to be making for a funeral service, days ago! Seriously, Miss... Amy? Please help me get out of here! I cannot let this person down again, I just can't!"

"Is there anything I can help you with? Speaking of which, we had no idea who to call the night you came in. Is there someone you'd like me to call?"

Panic raced throughout her body. Pure panic. Cam would be worried sick by now not knowing what was going on. She'd said she would let him know when she got to Maine and that call should have happened four days ago.

"My husband, Cam. Oh my God, he must be losing his mind about now! I need to call him. Do you know where my phone is?"

Amy went to the closet and retrieved the purse she had placed there days ago. Kallie called Cam, who was most definitely worried sick. She explained what she knew about the accident and tried to assure him that she was going to be fine.

"Jesus, Kallie! I'll be on the next flight out. I knew something must have happened for you not to call me. I've been a wreck. Thank God you are alive!"

"Honey, please listen to me. I appreciate you wanting to come home but I'm okay. I'm okay. There's nothing you can do for me here. This lovely nurse, Ms. Amy, is here with me taking excellent care of me. They all are. You couldn't do anything here anyway. Please stay and get this deal done before you come home."

"I don't care about a deal, Kallie. I care about you!"

"I know you care more about me than any deal, Cam.

And if there was anything you could do for me, I'd say come home. But there isn't. I will call you every day and let you know how I am; I promise. Please stay and do the purchase. For us. For me."

After she hung up the phone, she took a deep breath. She knew it wasn't going to be easy to convince him not to hop the first plane out of London. Fortunately, he had listened to her and agreed to stay to finish the deal. At least for now.

Amy was still in the room with her. "Someone loves you very much, I'd say!"

Kallie smiled. "He does. He's a good man. A great man. He's been working for a year or more on this big purchase deal in London. He wasn't happy about it but for the moment, I convinced him to stay and finish it up."

"He must mean an awful lot to you too." Amy added. "You were right. There is nothing he can do for you here. You're in great hands. We may be a small-town hospital, but we take pride in being a great one."

Kallie noticed that Amy wasn't wearing scrubs as the other nurses had been earlier that morning. "Are you not working today?"

"I'm not. It's my second, and last day off. I'll be back on shift tomorrow."

"What are you doing at work on a day off? I'm sure there's plenty to do on your time off rather than sit here visiting with me."

Amy laughed. "Well, this is exactly where I want to be. I wouldn't want to be alone through something like this and I didn't expect you would either."

Kallie didn't realize she had come in on a day off specifically for her. "You came in here on a day off *just* to see me?"

"I did. I'm glad to see you awake and feeling a bit better. I can see you have a bit of feistiness about you today and that's a good sign."

"Well, I must be doing *fantastic* then because I'm right sick of being tied to this bed. I meant what I said earlier. I do have some place to be. Looks like that's not going to be an option though, is it? I'll just have to figure out how I'm going to do everything I need to do from this bed."

Amy was glad to see that Ms. Douglas had come to terms with the fact that she wasn't going anywhere for the time being. "Ms. Douglas, is there something I can help you with? Anything at all?"

"Yes, there is, actually. Please call me Kallie."

Amy walked closer to the bed. "Kallie Douglas, it's nice to meet you. I'm Amy Wentworth."

Where had she recently heard that name? "Wentworth" sounded so familiar, but she couldn't place where she had heard it. "That name sounds so familiar. Have you and I met before, somewhere by chance?"

"I don't believe we have. But you did meet my husband the day before the accident. Maybe that's where you've heard the name? His name is Adam. Trooper Adam Wentworth."

Kallie laughed. "No kidding? I did meet him the night before the accident. He was so helpful and kind to a crazy lady bawling her head off in the breakdown lane."

Amy smiled a soft smile. "He's a kind man. The best but I may be a tad bit biased."

Kallie smiled back. What a small world it truly was. Of course, she was in rural Maine, where everyone knew their neighbors and doors were rarely locked. Maybe it wasn't that much of a reach to meet a police officer and days later, his wife the nurse. She could see them together. They both had an outward, caring personality. Perfectly fit for the careers they had chosen.

Kallie wished there were something the young woman could do for her. She really did. Was there some way she could completely erase the *crazy* that had been going through her mind four days ago? Could she make the nightmare of her childhood belong to someone else? She knew the answers. The Universe had given her all the break it was going to. There wasn't going to be anymore stuffing it away in the back of her head and pretending she didn't have things to sort out in her mind. It had become clear to her that she would have no peace, ever again, until she dealt with the memories head on. Good or bad, she couldn't hide from her past anymore and she knew it.

"Everything okay?" Amy asked as she noticed her staring at the wall ahead. Silent and deep in thought.

"Yes. I was just thinking that's all. I don't do the sit still thing very well and if I was rude to you earlier, I apologize. You've been so kind to me, and I really do appreciate it."

Amy dismissed the apology. "Oh, my goodness, no apology necessary. Trust me, I've had patients throw bedpans at me and anything else they can get their hands on. Trust me, you're a model patient! Besides, for days you've been silent."

They both laughed. Kallie decided she liked this woman. If she wasn't a patient in a hospital and she wasn't there to take care of her, they may have been friends. Maybe they could be. It didn't look like Kallie was going anywhere anytime soon. She was sure they would see plenty of each other in the next few days. Weeks most likely. She didn't have any idea how long she would be there, but it had already been much too long for her liking.

"You said something about surgery on my leg? What's

wrong with it? It's killing me right now, to be honest."

"I'd imagine it is. You have two breaks in your right leg, Kallie. My guess is that you'll have surgery on it sometime in the coming week now that you are conscious and breathing on your own. You do have a self-administer button somewhere there beside you, for the morphine. It should take the edge off the pain a bit."

Kallie laughed aloud. "So that's what it is? Morphine? I tried to ring the bell for help last night and thought it was weird that no one came. The next thing I knew I was all warm and fuzzy and floating around the room. No wonder no one answered the call bell!"

"That may explain it!" Amy laughed.

"Can I take you up on your offer to help me with something?"

"Absolutely! That's why I offered."

Kallie was beyond famished. The meal they had left for her earlier was about as bland as bland can get. No salt. No fat. No sugar. No taste. She was dying for something with flavor.

"No offense or anything, but the breakfast earlier was ... well...disgusting, to be honest. I'm so hungry. Is there some reason I can't have real food? With salt? Or sugar? Or flavor?"

Amy knew exactly what she meant. When a patient was able to eat, after surgery, the kitchen staff always sent a basic meal tray. "What sounds good? I'll see what I can get them to give me from the cafeteria."

"I'll take anything that I can taste, honestly. A peanut butter and jelly sandwich, I don't care."

Amy left for the cafeteria promising to scrounge something up with some flavor. Kallie reached for her purse, rifling through its contents until she found the notebook she knew was in there somewhere. She gently held the obituary she had printed off at home, in her hand as she read it over again.

Madeline O'Brien, lifelong resident of Maine, passed peacefully in her sleep at Pineview Hospital on August 9, 1997, from breast cancer. Madeline was well known throughout her community for her kindness and charitable acts. She is survived by her only child, Mrs. K. Douglas. Madeline will be remembered by the residents of Somerfield, Maine as a generous, loving person with the soul of an angel. A graveside service will take place at a later time. At Madeline's request, please consider donating to the American Cancer Society in lieu of flowers.

No matter how many times she read the short obituary, she couldn't help but wish there had been more written about Maddie's sacrifices and her never ending love and help of everyone she knew and even those she hadn't ever met. The woman was always doing something, always giving something of herself. Whether it was her time or the scarves and mittens she knit for the homeless community or teaching young people how to read at the local library, or baking goods for the local food cupboard, she was always selfless in her acts.

Not to mention what she had done for Kallie. The fact that she mentioned her as her child made Kallie smile. Even though she hadn't given the time to Maddie that she now realized she should have, it wasn't something Maddie held against her. She was an absolute angel in Kallie's eyes. Kallie knew there were others, many more, who felt the same.

Amy was back with a tray brimming with food. "The

head cook downstairs is a friend of mine. We grabbed a little of everything for you. Hopefully, something here will fill your craving."

"Oh wow! You are amazing! I thought you'd find a dry ole peanut butter sandwich or something! Look at this tray! Where to start? "

She felt like Christmas had come early. The ham and cheese sub with lettuce, cheese and tomato filled her up in no time.

"My eyes were bigger than my belly. I'm stuffed already." Kallie admitted.

Amy laughed. "Good! I'm glad you were able to eat something and actually taste it!"

"Are you this nice to all of your patients? If so, they are so lucky to have you at this hospital!"

"I do what I can to make people as comfortable as they can be while they are away from home. I have been so fortunate to meet many people and have learned so much along the way from my patients too. Speaking of which, I'm awfully glad to have been able to meet you, Kallie Douglas."

Kallie liked this girl. She was a kind soul like Madeline had been. That kind of character is something that you can't learn. Some people, very few people, are just born with a deep kindness that emanates from them without effort.

"Likewise, Amy. Sitting here chatting with you, I almost forgot I'm a prisoner to this bed. I do wish I could have skipped the accident part and had just met you elsewhere."

She looked at the obituary that laid beside her on the bed. She took the paper and held it out to Amy to read. "This is why I came back to Maine. An incredibly special lady has passed away and I was supposed to organize the memorial service for her. Only I didn't quite make it there."

Amy looked at the page feeling a little guilty that she had already been through Kallie's things and had already seen it.

"I need to let you know that I saw this a couple of days ago. I went through your bag looking for a name of family to contact. Someone I could inform of your accident. I didn't find one, of course, but I did look through your notebook also. I hope you can forgive me for being intrusive, Kallie. Please know that I wasn't being nosey, I truly was trying to help."

Kallie admired the honesty. "Oh, my goodness, Amy. Please get that look off your face and don't think another thought about it. You were doing your job for crying out loud. Of course, I'm not upset! I thank you very much for trying to find someone to call. Note to self: add an emergency contact and keep in purse!"

Amy laughed with her and looked down at the paper in her hand. "This woman must have been someone very special to you."

"She was. She was my guardian angel in human form, I tell you. I don't know what I would have done without her. I went to live with her when I was ten years old, and she changed my life. She saved my life."

"Aww. She sounds like a great person. Can I be nosey now and ask you how it came to be that you went to live with her? What happened to your parents?"

Kallie stared out the window beside the bed. Where to begin? How to answer that complicated question. How detailed should she get about the low life mother she had the misfortune to be born to? Should she answer at all?

After a few minutes of silence, she spoke. "Well, that's a complicated question requiring an even more complicated response. The long and short of it is that my biological mother decided she wanted one less child to take care of, I guess. When I was ten years old, she left me on a park bench to find another mother because she was no longer going to do the job."

Amy raised her eyebrows and gasped aloud. "Oh my God, Kallie. Are you serious? I'm so sorry. Wow! I guess I should have minded my own business. I had no idea. I'm really sorry."

"Don't be. It was the best thing that could have ever happened to me. I just didn't know it at the time. Madeline took me into her home and raised me like she would have one of her own. I *was* one of her own by the time I grew up. She saw me sitting there on that bench and never thought twice about doing anything less than all that she could give. Truly, truly, my angel."

She had a tear streaking down her face now. Amy knew it must have been difficult for Kallie to remember something so awful from her past. But at the same time, she felt good that this woman felt comfortable enough to share something like that with her.

"It sounds like you were truly fortunate to have had her in your life. I'm sorry to hear that she has passed on."

Kallie nodded. "I was very blessed to know her. I will call the attorney who is handling her affairs, probably tomorrow. He's no doubt wondering where I am by now. As soon as I'm out of here, I'll organize a memorial service and get started on cleaning out the house so it can be put up for sale."

"Sounds like you are going to have your hands full for a while. Please, Kallie. If there is anything I can do to help with any of this, don't hesitate to ask."

"Thank you, Amy. I can't tell you how much I appreciate what you've done and continue to do for me. I will certainly let you know if there's anything you can do to help."

Amy smiled. "Good. You know, there were many days when I was a child that I wished for a fairy godmother to drop from the sky and take me away from my own childhood. I'm glad to know they can be real!"

At some point, when she wasn't so incredibly exhausted, Kallie would have to ask about her childhood. As much as she wanted to continue the conversation, she could feel her eyelids becoming heavy. The next thing she knew she was asleep. Again.

Amy picked up the purse from the bed and reloaded its contents. Kallie was asleep once again and she was glad to see her resting. She would leave her a note for when she awoke letting her know she'd be back on duty tomorrow and for her to get some rest. Something about this woman made Amy feel close to her. Closer every time they spoke. She reminded Amy of who she had once wanted to be. A child rescued from a hellish home and given an opportunity to start over. Was that the connection she felt? Whatever it was, she was glad she was getting to know her better.

CHAPTER ELEVEN

As soon as Kallie awoke the next morning, she was told that she couldn't have breakfast since she would be going into surgery within an hour or so. She didn't even care about the lack of breakfast. First, she was tired of bland, tasteless food but more importantly, she would be on the way to healing once the surgery was over. Which was a good thing because she was jumping at the bits to get to planning Maddie's memorial service. Even though Attorney Miller had been more than sympathetic to her situation, as was the funeral home who had offered to keep Maddie's urn with them until she was back on her feet, Kallie was ready to get on with things.

Later that evening, Amy came in when she started her shift as had been her routine since Kallie had been admitted to Pineview. Kallie had dozed off, but Amy was glad to see her resting and relieved that the surgery had gone well. She knew what lay ahead for Kallie and she didn't blame her for wanting to get things moving. She would check back in later and not disturb her. Kallie had a long road ahead of her and Amy knew she'd need all the rest she could get.

****

The sound of dry branches snapping in the distance let her know that someone was behind her, moving through the trees. By the sound of the footsteps, they weren't far behind either. The faster she ran, the faster the footsteps hit the ground. There was no getting away! She stood behind the largest tree she could find, which was difficult to do in the pitch dark of the forest. Hopefully that tree would keep her from being discovered. With any luck, whoever it was would pass right by her and not know even she was there. Maybe if she could just hold her breath and not move a single muscle, she would be safe.

In the light of the moon, she could see the thick fog creeping in. A different sound was all around her now. Footsteps just the same but lighter; not as heavy. Not human footsteps she determined by the gentleness of each step. She peered out from behind the tree she that had tried to become part of and saw them. A small herd of whitetail deer, grazing from the forest floor all around her. She would be safe with deer. They weren't vicious animals, and they certainly weren't human, which made them all the safer in her mind. She could step out from her hiding place, and they would run. But they'd be running away from her not after her.

As she lifted a foot to step forward, she felt a hand on her shoulder from somewhere behind the tree. Panic raced through her veins. How had she not heard someone getting closer to her? How was she going to get away? And then she heard her. Maddie. She was in the distance calling her name. She had to yell. She needed to tell Maddie to stay away. Just like the last time she was there, she yelled but to no avail. It was as though she was silently yelling her head. She may as well have been imagining her voice crying out because no sound came out of her mouth each time she tried.

She had been here before, hadn't she? She tried hard to recall how to get out of this nightmare. As hard as she thought, she couldn't remember. All she could hear was the sweet sound of Maddie's voice calling out to her.

"No! Maddie! Stay where you are! It's not safe here!" she yelled. "Don't come over here, Maddie!"

"Kallie! It's okay. You're okay." she heard a soft voice assure her.

She opened her eyes to see Amy standing next to her bed.

"Amy! Oh, thank God it's you! I was having another bad dream. Maddie was there and someone was chasing me. Maybe it's the Morphine, I don't know but I've been having some weird dreams lately."

"That happens sometimes I hear. I also heard that your surgery went well and that is great news!" Amy beamed.

"Did it? I'm glad to hear that too!"

"Evidently you are now the proud owner of four titanium pins in your right knee and a brand-new kneecap to go along with them."

"Nice. I'll be hearing that bionic noise now when I jump over buildings!" Kallie laughed and realized that she had dated herself with the reference. One that Amy might not understand.

"Okay well maybe not but you *will* be able to walk. If you're a runner, you will be able to do that after a while too. You'll be staying with us for a few more days just to be sure everything looks good in there. Dr. Roberts wants to make sure you have a few more days to heal from your first surgery as well."

Kallie winked. "So, you're not kicking me to the curb just yet, huh?"

"Nah. We've grown kind of attached to you around here. We're going to keep you around as long as we can."

Amy left to see to other patients but promised to stop back in when she could. She wasn't gone five minutes when Kallie's phone rang. It was Cam. He was relieved to hear that surgery had gone as planned and that she would be on the mend going forward.

"So, you see, my love, it's a good thing you didn't come running back to the states. There was nothing you could have done for me. Plus, I'm doing fine."

"I know. You're a tough one my dear. You always have been. I'm glad to hear that they are taking such good care of you."

Kallie reassured him that she was being well cared for. "I can't say enough good things about this tiny little hospital, Cam. They have certainly gone beyond what I ever could have expected. One nurse has been amazing. Her name is Amy. I think we may be friends even after I'm released. She's been incredibly good to me. She's feels like a kindred spirit or something to me. We start talking and before we realize it, hours have flown by."

She could hear Cam smiling. "That's great honey. I'm glad there is someone there to talk to like that. Is she a Mainer born and raised?"

"I'm not sure. I think, but I don't know for sure. Weirdest thing happened though. She is the wife of the state trooper that I met that day on the highway. He was also the one who responded to the call the day of my accident. Small world huh?"

Cam laughed. "Small state. Small town. etc."

"That's true. Anyway, they are both really kind and caring people."

"I'm so glad to hear that babe. I think we should make sure that Pinewood Hospital understands how grateful we are for the care and compassion they've shown you. When I get back, let's talk about a sizable donation. Listen babe, I must let you go. Another meeting. I'm so glad you are doing better, and that the surgery went well. I'll call you this evening and we can chat a little longer, okay?"

"I will look forward to that. I love you, Cam."

"I love you beyond words my Kallie girl."

As she hung up, Amy returned with a tray of food. "Okay, so I went back to the cafeteria and grabbed whatever I could that wasn't low sodium or zero sugar. I intercepted a tray for you that I'd bet money had none of either since "Restricted "was written in large red letters on the tray tag."

"Oh! You are a peach, Amy! I am beyond starving and I don't think I could have stomached one more meal of that awful, restricted diet."

"I can't guarantee it's *delicious*, but maybe it's a little better than what was headed your way."

"I appreciate that, Amy. Speaking of food, I had the most amazing breakfast at the B&B here in town last week. Have you eaten there? Fresh popovers to die for, I tell you!"

"Aren't they though? Adam and I stop in for breakfast occasionally when we both happen to be off on the same weekend, which isn't often. Doris and Russell are the sweetest people you'll ever meet."

As Kallie devoured the French toast, a fruit bowl with oranges and melon, and coffee, Amy checked her vitals and disconnected the last intravenous line. Kallie wasn't sad to see that attachment gone.

"I love the little yellow ducks on your scrubs. Cute. I bet the kids like them too. I don't think I've even asked you if you have children. Do you?" Kallie asked.

Amy shook her head. "No. Having children isn't something I've ever really wanted to do. I think it's because of the way I grew up. My life was less than normal and that's putting it mildly. I think I've always been afraid I would turn out to be a mother like my own. No kid deserves that."

"How about you? Kids?"

Kallie laughed. "Oddly enough, no. And for the same reason you don't have any. I can't imagine voluntarily bringing a child into the world and risking them having a life like I did. I don't believe I am anything like my biological mother, but who knows. I have never been willing to risk it. Like you said, no kid deserves that. I feel the same about my mother."

"I know exactly what you mean. The sad part is my own mother doesn't think she did anything wrong. If you ask her, she was the model mother, and her children are just spoiled brats who never appreciated anything. I don't know, maybe that's what she has to tell herself to live with the things she's done."

"I wonder what women like that, your mother as well as mine, think? Do they set out to have children just to see how badly they can screw them up or is it just collateral damage along the way, while they are getting what they want from this world?"

Amy laughed. "Well, mine doesn't have one motherly bone in her body. Not sure why she didn't figure that out before she had us kids. She could have saved all of us a whole lot of hell if she had."

"How many siblings do you have?" Kallie asked.

Amy took the blanket from the guest chair and sat down. It was a slow day at Pineview, and she could take a minute to chat. She had learned to take breaks when it was quiet because that was apt to change in five minutes time, without warning.

"I'm the youngest of three."

"How about you? Siblings?"

"Oldest of four. Although I haven't seen them since I was ten years old and went to live with Maddie. I think about them a lot though and hope they have done well for themselves. If they have, they must have had to claw their way out of the hell hole they lived in with our mother. She is the kind of person who would be perfectly content to have all of them not amount to anything. Horrible, horrible woman she is."

"I hear ya. Mine too. The world rotates around her, for her, and only her in her mind. Mine never supported or helped any of us along the way. It was kind of every girl for herself, to be honest."

"Girls? No brothers either?" Amy asked.

"No Just four girls and her. I can't seem to call her mother. I just can't."

"That's too funny, Kallie. I feel the same about mine. I usually refer to her by her first name because the word "mother" gets stuck in my throat somewhere, refusing to come out."

Kallie could relate to that feeling wholeheartedly. "What about your dad? Was he around?"

Amy laughed. "I suppose he was around, somewhere, but not around his family. I don't ever think I met him. If I did, I must have been too young to remember him. I've never even seen a picture of him to tell you the truth. There weren't any in the house. I do remember my older sister asking about him once. That didn't go over too well. She got a whipping for that one. We were all told to never mention his name in her house or the same would happen to us. I never dared ask. None of us did. So, I don't know where he is to this day."

"Yours?" she asked Kallie

"Not really sure where he went. I remember him well, unfortunately. They were always getting drunk and fighting with each other. Sometimes even fist fighting. Then one day he took off. I heard rumors as a kid, that he had a girlfriend across town, but I don't know if that was true or not. He didn't come back home before I left. I'm not sure about afterward."

"Well, a fine kettle of fish we have here. Two strong women, raised by crazy people. Drunken people. Selfish, unable to love anyone but themselves kind of people. Yet here we are. I'd say we did all right for ourselves despite them and their craziness!"

Kallie held her hand out to Amy. "I've never thought of it that way, but you're right. If I weren't in this place right now, I'd take you out to celebrate US."

"If you weren't in this place, we wouldn't have met!"

They were laughing again. Too long and too loud for hospital etiquette, but it didn't bother them a bit. They were both old enough to know that some days there's not a whole lot in the world to laugh and enjoy. When there is, you embrace it. And embrace it they had for the afternoon.

"Did I miss a good joke?" a man's voice asked from behind the curtain.

Amy jumped at the voice. "Excuse me sir? Have you been eavesdropping? This *is* a private room you know!"

CHAPTER TWELVE

Adam stepped from behind the curtain. "Eavesdropping? I was doing no such thing Ma'am. I was at the nurse's station asking around for this beautiful nurse I've seen around here a time or two. That's when I heard the laughter, and I just followed the giggles."

Amy smiled. "Such a charmer my dear. Such a charmer. Kallie, you remember Adam, don't you?"

Kallie smiled. "I certainly do. Although I had no idea your wife was a nurse here at Pineview. Talk about a small world!"

Adam agreed. "That it is. Of course, I never expected you to meet Amy under these circumstances. I wish you had met another way, but still, I'm glad you two have had the opportunity to meet one another. Sounds like you've become fast friends."

Both women nodded their heads. "Your wife has been an absolute godsend to me while I've been here. Not only for the great company but I shudder to think what I might have had to eat. Don't tell anyone but this angel of yours, finds me food that actually has some taste to it."

Adam laughed. "Is that right? She's a good woman she is. I'll second that."

"What are you doing here during the day my dear? I thought you'd be sleeping for your shift tonight."

Adam shrugged his shoulders. "Well, you know how it is. Sound asleep and the phone goes off. I need to go in early tonight. Prisoner transport guy is out sick, so I'll be going south to pick up a prisoner for the county jail. Which is why I dropped by. I wanted to let you know I wasn't home."

"I appreciate that. But you could have texted me you know and saved yourself a trip over."

Adam blushed. "I know I could have. But I couldn't steal a kiss if I texted you."

Kallie liked the way they were still acting like school kids in love even after a few years together. She felt that way about Cameron too.

"You two are too freaking cute. Now get out of here and go say a proper goodbye to your handsome man. You two have reminded me that I need to call my husband."

"I'm very glad to see that you are feeling better Ms. Douglas." Adam called back toward her, as he was being dragged out of the room by his wife.

Kallie smiled as they left the room. She hadn't truly needed to call Cam since she had spoken to him earlier in the day. But she did need a minute to think. Talking with Amy about her childhood had brought up things that she hadn't thought of in such a long time. Things she hadn't planned on ever thinking of again. Although she hadn't known her for very long, it was easy to talk to Amy. Even about things she never imagined telling anyone besides Cam.

It sounded to Kallie that Amy could certainly relate because her stories of childhood didn't sound much different than her own. For so many years, she thought she was alone with her nightmares caused by a life that no child should have to live through. Listening to her nurse, she realized that there were a lot more people, a lot more children, going through less than normal lives, screwed up ones like she had known. She wondered if there were other families in town, that she never knew of, during her own childhood that were going through similar things.

Why was the craziness, the lack of food, the abuse, the alcoholism, all something that children knew were subjects they were not to speak of? She remembered clearly Connie pounding it into her head that what happened at their house was nobody's business but their own. If she had gotten wind that her daughters had been spreading rumors about what goes on in her house, she would have beat them half to death.

She had learned early on not to tell the secrets of the family. The more she thought about it, Kallie supposed there were many other children right in her town that had also learned that lesson from their own families. If she had realized that as a child, her life could have been different. The kids could have leaned one another for support. That's probably one of the reasons parents never wanted their secrets told. That and the fact that child services would have and should have, been involved in their lives.

Whatever the reason, Kallie felt somehow lighter for having shared what she did about her life. Somehow having spoken aloud about her abusive parents released some of the weight she had carried for so long. A painful weight that she hadn't really realized had been as heavy as it was. Maybe it was meant for her to be right there in that exact moment in time. She'd never been one to believe that our lives are determined by fate, as though people don't have a choice. Given the life she'd been born into, she knew without question, that there was always a choice. Still, she couldn't help but wonder if she weren't supposed to have had that crash and end up at Pineview, where she would meet Amy. Was this nurse was meant to help her deal with things from her past? Whether it was fate or something else, Kallie felt relieved to have been able to speak freely about the very things that had caused her to crash that car in the first place.

She pulled the blankets up around her chest and whispered, "I suppose stranger things have happened."

Sleep was coming easy to her these days, even without the Morphine drip that had been removed earlier. Kallie realized that for the first time in her adult life, maybe even her entire life, she was finally sleeping through the night. For as long as she could recall, she had always slept soundly for about one hour and would wake up abruptly. She always felt like she had woken from a bad dream, but never remembered what it was that had jarred her from sleep.

She slept through dinner that evening and before she knew it, the morning nurse was checking her vitals.

"Seriously? It's morning already? Not sure where yesterday went! "She laughed.

"I guess you must have needed the sleep. Breakfast will be here shortly."

Kallie wrinkled her nose. She sure wished Amy were on duty to bring her "real food," but her shift had ended a few hours ago.

The nurse on duty did have good news. "I have a surprise for you today, Ms. Douglas. After breakfast, we are going to take a walk down to the shower room and see how you do with that."

Kallie was thrilled. It had been days in that bed with nothing more than a sponge bath twice a day from the CNA. A real shower would be heavenly!

"That's the best news I've had in…well…since I've been here, to be honest!"

Finally! Some good news! If they were letting her make her way to the shower, she would hopefully hear news about a release date soon. She was ready for that. So much was riding on her recuperation. Maddie's service being first on her list of things to do. She certainly hadn't planned on *anything* being delayed for as long as it had. She would do what was right by her, she just had to get out of the hospital so she could get going on it.

A face she didn't recognize peered into her room. "Morning Ms. Douglas. I don't imagine you remember me, but I'm Dr. Roberts. I performed both of your surgeries."

"Oh! It's so nice to meet you, Dr. Roberts. I'd like to say thank you for taking such great care of me."

The doctor nodded and smiled. "You are most welcome. So how are you feeling after the last one?"

"I'm feeling pretty okay. The nurse just told me I am going to make my first attempt for the showers today, after breakfast. I'm ready!"

"I'm glad to hear that. Let's see how that goes and I'll stop back in tomorrow, and we can talk about a plan for your recovery."

"Sure. Thanks so much for stopping in and I look forward to discussing recovery as well as my release date."

"Sure thing. Let's take it one step at a time, though. Literally." he grinned.

Kallie laughed. A doctor with a sense of humor. She loved that. The communication from the staff was amazing. She honestly felt like she couldn't have been in better hands.

After her best attempt to finish off the tasteless breakfast of scrambled eggs and toast, Kallie was ready for her big trip to the shower. It was a slower and substantially more painful journey than she'd envisioned but she made it there and back and felt like a new woman afterward. A new woman with a brand-new knee and a geriatric walker, that is. Sleep came easy when she returned to her bed.

****

She was back in the forest. She knew she had been there before. She didn't want to be there. She felt lost among a sea of trees and a thick mist that covered the forest floor. Her loud heartbeat was the only sound she heard. Could it be heard pounding outside of her body too? Or did it just sound that way to her? She was afraid of something but couldn't remember what. One thing was for certain, she was terrified. But why?

Someone tapped her on the shoulder from behind and she re-membered all at once. Someone or something was after her, chasing her. Just like the last time she'd been in the nightmare. She couldn't bring herself to look back and see who it was. It didn't really matter who it was, her gut told her to run. Run as fast as she could. Small pine branches smacked her in the face with every step. Even though they burned like she had been whipped with a switch, she would not stop. She could not stop.

The fog was becoming thicker, and it was becoming harder to see even a foot in front of her. Which way was she supposed to go to get out of the maze of trees? Why couldn't she remember the way she had come in? Dammit, she'd been here before, which way did she go the last time? She looked toward the sky, hoping to recognize a tree, a branch, anything that would tell her what way she needed to go.

The footsteps were coming closer, and she couldn't get her feet to move any faster than they were already moving. Which was not fast enough. Every time she was there, in this dream, she could never seem to run fast enough. Whatever was coming for her seemed to al-ways be able to keep up with her.

Then she heard the voice. Maddie was calling her again. Each time she was there, she'd seen or heard Maddie, she was always try-ing to warn Maddie, but she never heard her for some reason.

"Maddie! I'm here! It's me! Kallie! Over here!" she yelled. But it wasn't a yell. It was barely a whisper. She couldn't raise her voice loud enough for anyone to hear no matter how she tried. Kallie knew that she needed to warn Maddie, but she couldn't get to her, and she couldn't hear her.

"Maddie, run! Maddie! Go Maddie! Go the other way!" she was yelling aloud from her bed. "Maaaddddiiieeee run!"

"Kallie? It's me, Amy. I think you were dreaming again. It's okay. Open your eyes, Kallie. Look. You are here at Pineview. It's just a dream. You're okay."

Kallie's forehead was drenched in sweat, and she was breathing so fast that Amy was afraid she was hyperventilating. She had her repeat after her, a slow breathing routine. Amy had never seen anyone awaken from a nightmare that frightened. She didn't care for the fast heart rate Kallie had awoken with either.

Kallie continued with the slowly paced breaths, calming down a little more as she did.

"Wow! That must have been some nightmare, girl. Your heart rate was insane there for a minute!"

"It's that same horrible nightmare, Amy. Someone's always chasing me. I can't see who it is, but I sense it's always the same person. Maddie is there too. Always. She's calling out to me, and I can't make a sound to warn her. Every time I open my mouth, barely a noise comes out. I'm in danger in the forest and she is too. Yet I can't stop her because she can't hear me telling her to run. Crazy how real it feels. As real as you and I sitting here talking.

Amy wiped Kallie's forehead with a cool cloth. "I hate those dreams that feel so real, even after you're awake."

Amy wondered if the nightmares had something to do with Kallie's guilt for not being there when Maddie passed away. She hoped that whatever the reason, they would get under control and disappear once Kallie was able to take care of Maddie's service and estate details.

"Feeling better?"

Kallie was grateful that it was Amy who had come into her room as she was waking up. Anyone else would think she was a lunatic. For some reason, she instinctively knew that Amy wouldn't think that of her. Or if she did, she hid it well.

"Much. Thank you so much. I can't tell you how much I appreciate you."

"My pleasure, Kallie, my pleasure. Listen, about the nightmare you keep having...Is it one that you've had for a long time and keeps recurring?"

"No. I don't believe so. I think I opened a can of worms by coming back here and somehow my subconscious is trying to tell me something? I don't know. I don't know what I believe about dreams and fate and that kind of thing."

"Dreams are hard to explain sometimes. I know when I left home and started out on my own, I had plenty of nightmares. Looking back, I was afraid of failure, and I think that's what the dreams had formed from. Thankfully, that was years ago now and I fortunately don't have them anymore."

"That's a good thing they have stopped for you. Seriously, Amy, it was like cracking open a time capsule or something when I crossed the border into Maine. I haven't been back here for so long and it's like once I did, every past thought, feeling and emotion hit me all at once. The Universe is telling me it's time to deal with things and it's doing it's damnedest to make sure I can't ignore the message."

Amy smiled. "Yep. The Universe sure has a way of making sure we listen when it's important doesn't it? The good news is that you are on the road to healing now physically. The rest will follow. You seem like a smart lady to me. I've no doubt you will deal with whatever needs tending to and you will be all the stronger for it."

"I hope you're right, Amy. I really need for this to stop so I can move on. I have so much to do as soon as I get out of here, as you know."

For the next few days, Amy continued to stop by and chat with Kallie as much as she could. Sometimes it was the middle of the night when all the other patients were asleep, that they would visit. It was a perfect time for Amy to take a break and Kallie couldn't sleep well, so she always appreciated the company.

She'd learned so much about Amy during those wee hours of the night visits. Turns out, they both had the determination of a small army when it came to making something of themselves. Amy also had felt the need to prove that she was worthy enough to be someone after a lifetime of getting zero support and listening to a mother who put her down constantly. Kallie could certainly relate to that. They had become friends and Amy's friendship was something that Kallie valued more during her time in that bed, than Amy would ever know.

Cameron called every day, sometimes many times a day, and he too was relieved that his wife had someone there to confide in. When his business in London was finished, he vowed to meet the woman who had done so much for his wife. Kallie had always been a strong woman but for the first time in years, he was glad to hear that she was working through some of the memories she had chosen to bury so long ago. It sounded to him like her new friend was instrumental in facilitating that and he was beyond grateful.

CHAPTER THIRTEEN

Two weeks after landing upside down in the gorge, and becoming a resident at Pineview Hospital, Kallie received word that she would be released. Finally. She was itching to get out of that bed and get to work on Maddie's affairs. The staff had been beyond friendly and accommodating to her and she would never have anything but wonderful things to say about them. Still, it was time for her to go.

Dr. Roberts explained that even though she was leaving the hospital, she would not be able to leave the area just yet. She had a few weeks of physical therapy ahead of her. He was perfectly clear and frank with Kallie regarding the orders not to travel back to Virginia. If she couldn't assure him that she was not going to leave the Somerfield area, he would not be signing her release papers.

Kallie assured him that she would not be leaving. She would contact Doris and Russell over at the B&B and see if there was a room available. It was the perfect location as it was close enough to get back and forth to Pineview for her physical therapy appointments. She also had two additional MRI's scans scheduled for the coming weeks to be sure the new hardware was doing well.

She promised and intended to do whatever the doctor told her to do if it meant getting out of the bed. She felt like she won the lottery. Finally, she could get on with the business of Maddie's funeral service. She couldn't wait to contact the funeral home and let them know she was ready to talk about planning the service Maddie so deserved.

Amy poked her head in the door. "What are you doing here

Ms. Amy? I know it's a day off for you! You should be doing something fun not hanging around here!"

"Well, a little birdie told me that a certain someone is being released today. I couldn't think of a place I'd rather be than celebrating the good news with her!"

Kallie smiled. "I'm glad you're here! I really am! I can't believe it's finally happening! Not that you all haven't been the most wonderful people to me, but I'm ready to run out the front door as fast as I can. Which evidently wouldn't be fast with this big ole clunker of a cast!"

Amy completely understood. "I don't blame you! You've been through a lot in the past few weeks but it's good to see you feeling better. Every day going forward you will feel more and more like your old self again."

Kallie wondered if that was true. "I don't know about my old self, but maybe by the time I get back to Virginia, I'll have dealt with a lot of things I never wanted to, and I can be a new/old, improved version of myself."

Amy knew exactly where Kallie was coming from. She had reluctantly undergone the same transformation after her split from Jared. For herself, she also believed the Universe was sending a message that she knew she'd better listen to. Now, she was glad she had. Otherwise, she may not have found someone like Adam at all. More than likely, she would have kept repeating the pattern of being with someone who didn't deserve her.

"And Dr. Roberts explained to you that you can't leave the area just yet?"

"He did. I am so excited to leave the hospital, I don't even care that I need to stay in Somerfield. I need to be here anyway so I can take care of things with Maddie's estate. So, it's a win- win as far as I can see."

"That's true. So where are you planning on staying?"

Kallie was sitting on the bed fidgeting as she waited for the charge nurse to bring her release papers to sign. "I was thinking I would stay at the B&B. I'm going to call Russell and Doris and see if they would have room for me for a couple of weeks. I could stay at Maddie's house, but honestly, I don't want to stay there by myself. Too many memories. Besides, the bedrooms are all upstairs and I don't think I'll be running up and down the stairs just yet." she laughed.

"Why don't you come stay with Adam and me? It's just the two of us in a four-bedroom house. We would love to have you!" Amy offered.

Kallie didn't know what to say. Adam and Amy had already done so much for her in the short time since she'd met them. There was no way she wanted to impose on them further. Still, she thought it amazingly generous that they had offered.

"Oh, my goodness! No! Thank you so much for the invite. I mean it. But you and your husband have done so much for me already. You two have lives of your own and I'm sure the last thing you need is me hobbling around in your way!"

Amy shook her head. "Don't be silly, girl! We haven't done anything we haven't wanted to do. I already spoke to Adam about this briefly last night when I heard you were going to have a visit from Dr. Roberts this morning. We both would love to have you come to stay with us."

"What? You knew last night, and you didn't share?" Kallie laughed.

"Nope. I wanted you to enjoy the surprise. Besides, it makes much more sense to stay with us. You will have therapy appointments and all that you have to do with Madeline's estate. I can drive you where you need to be."

"Have you forgotten that you have a job and sleep days to work nights as does your husband but on different shifts?"

Amy laughed aloud. "No. I haven't forgotten but I also didn't tell you that I'm on vacation for the next two weeks. So, you see, it's perfect timing!"

"You are? Seriously? Amy, I don't know what to say. Are you both sure? I know it would be weird to have another person around when it's always been the two of you."

"Not weird at all! So there, it's settled. Have you let your husband know that you're being released yet?"

"I haven't! I had just finished speaking with the doctor when you came in. I better call him and let him know right now. Thank you so much for asking me to stay with you. I still think I'll be an imposition, but I will gladly take you up on the offer, if you're certain it's no problem."

Amy laughed. "No problem. Now, call your honey and let him know about your plans. I'll see if I can track down those release papers for you."

Kallie held out her arms. "You are a wonderful person, Ms. Amy. I have never quite had a friend like you."

As she returned Kallie's hug, she said, "Neither have I, my friend. Neither have I."

+++++++++

Kallie voiced her dislike of having to leave the hospital by way of a wheelchair, but she decided that arguing with the stern looking charge nurse, wasn't a clever idea. As Amy's car pulled out of the hospital parking lot, Kallie felt a huge relief. She was finally free of the bed that she felt had held her prisoner for weeks. She could walk, although slowly, with the crutches. She knew that getting around would be a bit of a struggle, but it was going to be so much better than lying in bed.

She had spoken to Cam just before signing the release papers. He so desperately wanted to come back to the states and take her home. He still had a couple more weeks in London and Kallie encouraged, or rather demanded, that he fulfill his obligations there. She explained that she would be staying with Amy, the nurse. This made him feel much more relieved than the idea of Kallie staying all alone at a Bed & Breakfast. She promised to continue to contact him every day and let him know how she was doing. She would also update him regularly regarding the progress she had made with Maddie's estate.

Just a few miles out of town, they turned onto a gravel road that reminded Kallie of a scene from a childhood fairy tale. The largest maple trees she had ever seen formed a thick canopy over the entire road. The countless shades of multiple greens appeared to have come from an artist's brush. She felt like she was riding through a tunnel. Bright sunlight poked through the trees illuminating spots along the road where they saw two wild rabbits lounging in the warm sun.

"Wow! This is your drive home every day?" Kallie asked.

"It is. Isn't it amazing? I never get tired of the scenery."

Soon they pulled into a driveway lined with Pine trees. As they made the uphill climb, Amy said, "Just around one more corner and we're home."

When they crested the hill, Kallie was in awe at the most beautiful log home she'd ever seen. Tucked between the pine and fir trees, proudly stood the two-story beauty adorned with a full front porch. Two chairs constructed from pine logs and a matching bench gave a welcoming feel. She never knew a log cabin could be so majestic, but this one surely was.

"So, this is it." Amy said, "This is where we call home."

"Amy, I don't know what to say! This house, this spot, it's like something out of a magazine. I don't believe I've ever seen any-place more beautiful."

"Thank you, Kallie. We really like it here. You know, Adam built this place with his own two hands. Every piece of wood used to build the house was taken right from this land."

Kallie was impressed. "No kidding? Wow! He's not only a kind and generous law enforcement officer but he can build too! I *am* impressed!"

Amy nodded. "That was my response when I saw it for the first time, too. C'mon, I'll show you the inside. Stay right there though until I come around and help you. We don't need you falling and going back to Pineview!"

Once they made it up the front steps, Kallie scooted toward one of the wooden chairs. The trip from the car had taken more out of her than she expected. "Thank God there's only four steps. I don't think I could have made five!"

Amy completely understood. "You'll get a little bit stronger every day. You'll see."

After catching her breath, they made their way into the house. Just inside the entryway, Kallie stood taking in the breathtaking sight. She had never been inside a log cabin before that had been truly a log cabin built from the land it sat on. And she certainly didn't know anyone that lived in one as gorgeous as the one she was seeing with her own eyes.

A tall cathedral ceiling seemed to go upward into the tree-tops that shown through the glass ceiling panels. The entire interior was hand-hewn logs, protected with a polyurethane sealant that shone in the light. An upstairs loft ran around the entire outside of the cabin with a beautiful staircase leading up to it. Framed photographs of Maine wildlife adorned the walls throughout. A field stone fireplace stood in the center of the house. One side was the living area with a love seat and two matching chairs. On the other side of the fireplace was a dining area and kitchen. Beautiful gray and white granite lay across the maple cabinets in the kitchen area.

This place is something else!"

"Thank you, Kallie. I'm so glad you like it. When Adam and I met, it was nothing more than a shell of a building. Together we finished it off inside and made it a place for us to call home."

Amy helped her to the overstuffed love seat and helped her to get comfortable before she went to the kitchen to make a pot of coffee.

"Ahh, this is heaven, Amy! I feel like this chair is giving me a bear hug! I don't know if I ever want to move again!"

"Good. I'm glad you feel at home!"

It was hard not to feel the coziness of the place. As she looked around, Kallie noticed that every decoration had a thread of Maine wildlife running through it. The attention to detail was perfect. Even the curtains were rustic yet magnificent. It was obvious that their home was a place that was important to both Adam and Amy.

Amy returned with two mugs of coffee. Kallie was thrilled to have home brewed coffee again. "No offense but this tastes like coffee. What they serve at Pineview, I'm not sure what it is to be honest, but it doesn't taste much like coffee."

Amy laughed. "Couldn't agree more. I am grateful for the "Pineview Brew" when I need a surge of energy on a long shift, but it's not something I would choose to have, otherwise, that's for sure."

Kallie nodded in agreement. "I don't know how you health-care providers survive on that stuff. Tastes like week old coffee that they watered down about fifty times! Speaking of staff... there's something I was wondering about but forgot to ask you the last time we were chatting about life."

"Oh? Well, ask away my friend. Ask away!"

"I was wondering what it was that made you want to be a nurse. I suppose there's a reason we all end up going into the careers we do; I was curious about why you chose yours."

Amy tilted her head as she thought. "Hmmm. Well, I suppose the reason is because I wanted to help people. I didn't come from a background where I saw a lot of help, apart from my mother, who helped herself and no one else. So, I wanted to do something that would benefit others."

"Well, I for one, am sure glad you made that decision!"

"Thank you. I wanted to become something that was at the opposite end of the spectrum as she was...is. That was probably always in the back of my subconscious mind somewhere."

"I can certainly understand that! I wanted to run away as far as I could from Somerfield. I wanted to prove to every single person I ever met that I was nothing like Connie! I wasted a lot of time. I see that now. In reality, I had no one to prove anything to. I am not her and I never will be."

Amy sat with a puzzled look on her face. "Connie? Is that your mother's name?"

"Well, the woman who gave birth to me. That's her name, yes. As far as I'm concerned, Maddie was all I ever knew for a mother."

"You're not going to believe this, Kallie but my mother's name is also Connie."

Kallie laughed. "Well, it must be something in the name that makes both yours and mine a couple of selfish witches!"

Amy laughed. "I think you may be right! She is a witch all right. She's much worse than that, but I've given up thinking of new names for her. She just is what she is and that won't ever change."

"No. People like that rarely do. Imagine that?! Two women, both from the Somerfield area, both named Connie. And they both happen to be our mothers!"

Amy almost choked on her coffee. "I know it! Oh my God, Kallie, I wonder if they know one another? Wouldn't that be something?"

They both laughed hysterically at the idea. In between giggles, Kallie managed to get out, "Can you just imagine if they do? Oh my God, that would be insane!"

"Yeah, it would. No doubt, by the sounds of them, they'd be best friends if they did!"

"On the other hand," Kallie said, "Mine seemed to prefer *male* drinking buddies. She never did have many female friends. So maybe not."

"Mmmhmm Mine always had a fondness for the slimiest men friends also. I'm sure they were just funding her drinking habit, but oh Lord were they nasty!" Amy recalled as she sipped from her mug. "My father wasn't much better, truth be told. He was only around for the welfare money and then he took off when it was gone."

Amy stood to refill her cup and grabbed Kallie's on the way by. She knew her well enough by now to know that she would want a refill, there was no need to ask. They also had a love of coffee in common, she'd learned.

Amy called from the kitchen, "I'm sure my father wasn't any better either, Kallie. If he were anything worth mentioning, she would have told me about him. I assume he was flat broke, or she would have kept him around. Oh, she did compare me to him once. She was mad at me because I spent so much time at the library. She wanted me home to do her dirty work around the house. Trust me, I could have cleaned that place twenty-four seven and that dump never would have come clean. Anyway, she was scolding me for going to the library after school one day. She told me there was no point in trying to be something that I wasn't ever going to be. Albert Jansen's daughter wasn't going to amount to a "piss-hole in the snow" anyway. That was the only time I ever remember her saying his name to me."

CHAPTER FOURTEEN

There was silence from the living room. Amy wondered if Kallie had fallen asleep on her as she rattled away from the kitchen. She grabbed both mugs and headed for the love seat. Kallie was sitting on the couch with her head in her hands shaking her head back and forth.

"Kallie? You okay? Do you want to lie down? I know it's been a busy day for you being the first day out and all."

Kallie looked up at her. She had tears streaming down her face. Her hair stuck to the warm tears against her cheeks. Amy slowly bent over and placed the mugs on the coffee table.

"Kallie? What is it?"

"Say it again, please?" Kallie muttered.

"I don't understand. Say what again?"

"What did you say your father's name is?"

Amy looked her not fully understanding what was going on just yet.

"Well, he wasn't a father to me as I told you…he wasn't around, and I never met him but evidently his name was Albert Jansen. Why?"

Kallie grabbed the throw cushion from beside her and buried her face in it as she cried. Amy had absolutely no idea what was going on. Was Kallie having a full-blown mental breakdown? Had she heard the name? Nothing was making sense. Kallie continued to wail from behind the throw pillow.

"Kallie? Please tell me what I can do to help you. I don't know what's going on, I really don't. If you tell me, maybe I can help you in some way. Please talk to me."

Kallie didn't know what she was supposed to say. There was no way Amy was going to believe what she was about to tell her. Should she tell her? She didn't know if it would help or hurt Amy. She had worked so hard to put things behind her and move on with her life without from her mother, just as Kallie had. Would telling her that she had found the one in a million person in the world that could be her sister, help or hurt? She didn't know what was best at that moment. All she could do was cry. She had found her baby sister, Amy. Or at least she was semi-certain she had. A mother named Connie. Albert Jansen was her father. There was no way she couldn't be her sister, was there? Was this woman's birth name Amaretta? Should she ask? It was the only way she was going to know for sure.

She pulled her face from the pillow and grabbed a tissue from the box on the coffee table. She took a deep breath and spoke. "Listen to me, Amy. This is especially important. I need to ask you something else."

Amy kneeled in front of her. "Of course. Please, ask me whatever you want. However, I can help, I will!" She reached for Kallie's hand and held it in her own.

Another deep breath. She looked Amy directly in the eyes and said, "Was your birth name Amaretta?"

Amy about fell backwards into the coffee table. She reached for the arm of the love seat to steady herself. No one had called her that since childhood. Other than Adam, no one knew that was her given name. No one.

"How? How did you? How would you, know that?"

"Are you saying yes?"

"Yes, Kallie. That is my birth name but how could you know that? No one knows that name except Adam and I can't imagine he would have told you that the one time you talked to him."

Kallie reached for Amy and hugged her as she cried. "Amy, my birth name was Kahlua Jansen. My parents are Connie and Albert Jansen!"

Amy felt her grasp free from Kallie's arms as she fell backward onto the floor landing on her bottom. "What? I mean, what? Are you kidding me?"

Kallie wiped her eyes with the back of her hand. "I am dead serious, Amy. Dead serious!"

"I don't understand. How? How can that be? I mean, I have two older sisters named…"

Kallie interrupted and finished her sentence. "Ginger and Brandy. Ginger is two years older than you and Brandy is five years older. Right?"

It was Amy who could not stop crying now. She pulled her knees to her face and cried like she'd never cried before. How could this be? How could this woman that she had just met a few weeks earlier, be her sister? Why would she have not known about this? Why had no one told her about Kallie? There had to be some mistake. There just had to be. Things like this didn't happen in real life, did they? Did they?

She looked at Kallie, who was reaching for another tissue and handing it to her.

"Okay, there has to be some mistake. As much as I'd love for you to be a long-lost sister that I never knew I had, that's crazy. Right? I mean, how would I not have known about you?"

"Yes. It does sound crazy, Amy. I agree. I know your sisters' names and ages because I am the oldest of Connie's daughters."

Amy shook her head. "No way. I mean, just no way!"

Kallie continued. "Okay. You remember when I told you

about how it was that I came to live with Maddie?"

Amy shook her head. "I do."

"Well, that was because Connie, our mother, dropped me off on that bench! When I left that day, Brandy was six, Ginger was three and you had just turned one."

Amy was confused and Kallie understood that she had every right to be. If it hadn't been the truth of her own life she was telling, she too would have thought it was a fictional story or an outright lie. But it wasn't fiction, and it wasn't a lie. It was her past. Her life. And now, it was part of her sister's life too.

"But no one and I mean no one, ever once in my entire life mentioned you. Not ever! Wouldn't the other girls have at least mentioned you if you were our sister?"

Kallie smiled. "What happened when you did something that went against whatever Connie told you to do or not to do?"

"We were spanked. Which truthfully, seemed to be a regular occurrence now that I think of it." Amy answered.

"Exactly. I don't know if Ginger would have remembered me, but I guarantee you that Brandy was threatened within an inch of her life if she ever told either of you about me."

Kallie was speaking the truth about that. Amy knew that to be exactly the way it had been living in that house.

"Brandy is Connie's sidekick. She does and always did what she told her to do. If Connie wanted us spanked and was too drunk to do it herself, she would tell Brandy to do and she did!"

"Jesus! She turned out just like her, didn't she?"

"Oh, she did. She never even left home. It was like she just gave up trying to be something good, something different than Connie. Something happened, and I don't know what, but something happened when Brandy was about twelve or so that made her into a monster. And I mean that literally. She became the walking, talking younger version of Connie Jansen."

"Well, probably better if you don't know what happened to make her change like that. Nothing good, that much is for sure!" Kallie added.

Amy sat on the floor cross legged and reached for her coffee. "Jesus, Kallie. Is this true? I mean, what are the odds? You end up in the hospital that I work in. I take care of you, and we become friends. You're sitting here in my home right now. And we are sisters? Can this truly be real?"

Kallie held out her arms to her sister and they sat crying and laughing and then crying and laughing some more. She realized, at that moment, that fate had played a hand she never saw coming. And she couldn't be happier for it. Kallie knew, at that moment, that she had been right the other day when she wondered if the Universe had sent her to Pineview on purpose. Pineview Hospital where she was supposed to meet this woman, who had become her friend. She was certain of it. She had been sent, in a roundabout way. Of course, she wished she could have come without having to endure an auto accident, to find her baby sister. But either way, she had found her. That was the important thing.

"The world is a funny place, Amy. Never in my wildest imagination did I ever think I'd run into one of my sisters. And I certainly wouldn't have seen it coming by way of an automobile accident that almost took my life!"

"Wait until Adam hears this! He is not going to believe it! I can barely believe it myself!"

Kallie laughed. "No, me either. I keep thinking it can't be true, but I know it is. Cam is going to flip his lid when he hears this! There's no way he's going to believe it when I tell him. He already thinks Maine is a small place, just wait til he hears how small!"

After they finished their coffees, Kallie suddenly felt completely exhausted. It had been a full day for sure. One that she would never in her life forget. She also was realizing she wasn't as physically strong as she would like to be. She understood that it would take time and she was all right with that. Whatever time it took, she would do it. She was safe in Maine with her baby sister, the nurse, to look after her. Nothing was ever going to look too hard to handle ever again. Nothing.

"Amy, I hate to be a buzz kill, but girl, I am exhausted."

Amy stood to help Kallie to her feet. "I bet you are! I have been so completely wrapped up in this news, our news, our great news, that I totally forgot you were just released from the hospital a few hours ago! You must be tired! C'mon, I'll show you to the guest room."

Kallie slowly followed Amy down the hallway, just past the kitchen, to the guest room.

As Amy opened the door, Kallie smiled. Inside the room stood a four-poster bed, also made from pine logs, with a canopy over the top. Clear, white miniature twinkle lights illuminated the outline of the headboard. A patchwork quilt in multiple shades of green covered the mattress. In the corner, a small tree trunk table with a thick piece of glass held a lamp made from driftwood. It would have been impossible to not be comfortable in the room.

Amy helped her to the edge of the bed, and left the room, promising to be right back. She came in waving a blue and white tote bag that looked like it was a bit worse for wear.

"I thought you might want this. It's all that was salvageable from the wreck. There's not much in there, but tomorrow or whenever you feel like it, we can get you some new clothes. In the meantime, I've plenty of comfy pajamas you can borrow."

Kallie looked inside and laughed aloud. She reached into the bag, pulled out a piece of clothing, and held it high into the air as though she had found buried treasure.

"Hey! My favorite pj's survived the accident! That's all I really cared about anyway!"

Amy laughed. "Nothing like a good ole pair of cozy jammies is there?!"

Amy opened both windows on either side of the bed, letting fresh air into the room. Kallie loved the way the curtains were gently dancing on the summer breeze that drifted into the room. Amy had barely left the room when Kallie felt her eyelids drooping. The songs from the chickadees lulled her to sleep in no time.

CHAPTER FIFTEEN

The comforting aroma of coffee filled her nostrils as she began to wake. For a minute, Kallie forgot that she wasn't at home in her own bed. As she opened her eyes to the sunlight streaming in the window, and remembered she was at Adam and Amy's house. She began to recall the conversation she and Amy had before she dozed off. It *was* real and not a dream, wasn't it? The way her mind had been lately, she wasn't completely sure.

Amy was her sister? The nurse who had been taking care of her in the hospital was her sister. What were the chances of something like that happening in real life?

Cam was not going to believe her news. She wouldn't blame him, truthfully. She barely believed it herself. She knew she needed to call him and fill him in. Although, part of her wondered if she was connecting dots that weren't there. She wanted to run the conversation past him and get his thoughts on all of it. He had a way of keeping her focused. If she were just wishing the entire thing to be true, he would point that out to her. The man had a way of steering her in the right direction and she loved that about him. At times when her compassion and empathy for a situation overshadowed logic, Cam could always keep her on track.

Amy knocked as she opened the door and walked into the guest room. The call to Cam would have to wait until after breakfast. Amy came bearing a plate of pancakes that Kallie wasn't about to turn down.

"Knock! Knock! Anybody home?" Amy teased as she walked into the room. "I thought you might be hungry."

"I can't believe I slept through the entire night! It was late afternoon when I came in to lie down. Guess I was more tired than I realized. And yes, I'm starving!"

"Well, you had quite a day yesterday. Getting freed from the hospital AND finding out that your nurse is your sister! I'd imagine that would tire anyone one out!"

"So, I wasn't dreaming? We really *are* sisters, right? I woke up a few minutes ago wondering if I had dreamed it."

Amy laughed. "Nope. Not a dream. I still can't believe it's real either, but it is! I couldn't be happier that it is, by the way!"

Kallie threw her a soft smile. "And we're not just trying to make connections that aren't there, right?"

Amy laughed. "I'm afraid not my dear. Our mother is Connie Jansen. Our father is Albert Jansen. My birth name is Amaretta Jansen and yours is Kahlua Jansen. Seems pretty cut and dry to me."

"Oh, it's not that I don't want it to be true, Amy. I would love nothing more. It's just that lately, since I came back here, I have been haunted by bad memories. So much so, that I wasn't clear if it was just something I was wishing for or if it was real."

"Quite understandable, Kallie. I waited up for Adam to come home last night. I couldn't wait to tell him and see his reaction."

"I bet! What did he say when you told him?"

"At first he thought I was joking with him. By the time I told him our parents' names and the part about your being left on the park bench, I thought the man was going to cry. He's so happy for us!"

Kallie was glad that Amy had the support of a man like Adam. It made her feel warm inside to know that at least one of her siblings had done well for herself. She had made a life giving back to others as a nurse and had finally found the love she deserved in Adam.

"He must have been shocked! Amy, I want you to know that I am so happy to see that you have a good life. I always wondered about how you girls were doing. I knew if you succeeded in life, it was going to be damned hard to get away from Connie's grasp. I can't even imagine the strength it took for you to not let her ruin your dreams. I'm so proud of you!"

Amy's eyes filled with tears. "Listen to you! It is I who am amazed at *you*! You were the one abandoned when you were just a little girl! The fact that you managed to make a decent life for yourself is beyond admirable!"

Amy sat the breakfast tray on the bed and reached over to give Kallie a hug.

"I never imagined I'd ever meet any of my sisters ever again. This is the best thing that has happened to me since meeting Cam all those years ago. I can't tell you how much I've missed not knowing you!"

"We have a lifetime of catching up to do, Kallie. But right now, you have a lot of other things you need to take care of. I want you to know that I'm here to help you with whatever I can. You are not on your own and don't have to do anything on your own okay?"

"I can't tell you how much that means to me."

They hugged and cried until Kallie's phone went off. "That must be Cam. I was going to call him after breakfast. I have a lot to fill him in on, huh?"

"I'd say you do. Let me set this tray over here on the night-stand and you can nibble when you want. Afterward, I can help you wrap the leg so you can shower, okay? *Sis?*"

It was the first time Kallie had heard anyone call her that since she was ten years old. She was overcome with emotion as she answered the phone. The simple word, "sis" was one that meant so much to her to hear aloud. One that she hadn't even realized she missed until that moment. Kallie spoke with Cam for over an hour. He was as much in disbelief and shock as she and Amy had been at the revelation that they were not only friends but sisters.

Cam was relieved to hear that his wife was having an opportunity to spend time with a sister that she'd never known. He couldn't help but wonder if she'd been right when she said that the Universe led her to that accident and everything that followed, so that she could find Amy. He never believed much in the things that people said were "meant to happen" but this situation was hard to think of in any other way. He hadn't heard Kallie so excited about something in years. Maybe not ever. When he returned home, he would be anxious to meet his new brother and sister-in-law. They had given him a great peace of mind by taking care of the love of his life when he couldn't be there. He knew there would never a way to repay them that would ever be sufficient.

Amy wrapped the cast so that Kallie could shower. She had limited mobility, but she was managing to do things for herself, quite well. The hot water was soothing as it ran over the bruises on her skin. Kallie had forgotten how nice it was to have the ability to do something as simple as taking a shower on her own. A task that she had always taken for granted until she wasn't able to do it any longer.

She had spoken to Amy earlier about the things on her list that needed to be done regarding Maddie's service, the house and all that followed. Her sister reiterated her offer to help with anything she could, and Kallie took her up on it. She needed to go to Maddie's house. She hadn't stepped foot inside the house since leaving for college all those years ago. It wasn't something she was looking forward to she realized. It was not going to be the same house without Maddie in it. Still, Kallie knew it was something she had to do. It was something she couldn't put off any longer. Attorney Miller had phoned the day before and asked her to try to find the life insurance policy that Maddie had mentioned to him. Maddie had never gotten around to bringing it to his office before she passed away.

The life insurance payout would be rolled over into a scholarship fund for low-income students residing in the town of Somerfield. Kallie loved the idea and was so proud of Maddie for wanting to create a scholarship to help children who needed it. It was just another one of the selfless ways she had always thought of other people. That was her Maddie. Selfless, loving, and ready to give her last penny to someone who needed it more.

+++++++++

Amy pulled into the driveway and Kallie felt her heart doing cartwheels inside of her chest. Mixed feelings of homesickness and comfort took hold throughout her body. The house was small, painted beige with white gingerbread trim adorning the eaves. It was the only place she had laid her head, as a child, that truly felt like home. A cobblestone walkway led the way to the welcoming front door. She lifted the fourth Marigold pot at the end of the walk, hoping to find the spare key. She was happy to see that Maddie had never changed her hiding place.

Opening the front door, she was hit by the familiar scent that was nowhere else in the world but there. It was the scent of "home." A combination of every meal Maddie had ever cooked mixed with hints of lavender. Every vase in the house held lavender. Dried lavender, fresh lavender, even lavender scented candles. The woman loved lavender and called it natures miracle healer. She was convinced the relaxation, calming effects of the purple herb could cure whatever ailed a person.

Everything looked the same as the day she had left for Mt. Vernon University. The cast iron wood cook stove still stood along the back wall of the kitchen and the wooden claw foot table and it's six matching chairs filled the dining area.

She hadn't been in the house five minutes when she felt the tears welling up behind her eyelids. Maddie's presence was everywhere, and she so badly wished she was too. There was Maddie's favorite chair, where she had sat so many evenings knitting mittens for the neighborhood children. There was her favorite painting of the Maine coast that Maddie's grandfather had painted so many years earlier, still hanging on the living room wall. For a moment, she could still see herself with Maddie as they sat at the card table playing board games during the long Maine winter nights. She sat down on the mustard yellow sofa and let herself feel what the house was telling her. Deep in thought, she simply allowed herself to cry. Amy kept her distance, sensing that it was something her sister needed to handle on her own.

Trying to be as quiet as she could, Amy began to pack the China from the antique cabinet in the dining room. Kallie had mentioned it would be something that she would keep as it had been Maddie's grandmother's China. As a young girl, she had listened each time, as though it was the first, as Maddie told her how it had been handed down to her and how it would go to her daughter one day. She always said Kallie was the daughter she had prayed for and one day she would give it to her to display in her own home.

The thoughtful consideration of space that Amy had

given meant so much to Kallie. When she was ready, she asked Amy to help her to the second floor. She'd attempted to make a go of the steep stairs alone but thought better of it.

Kallie sat on the bed in her childhood bedroom surveying the items she had left behind so long ago. Everything was exactly as she had left it. Posters of her favorite eighties "hair" bands still hung on the wall. The jewelry box with the spinning ballet dancer, a Christmas gift from Maddie her first year there, was still sitting on the dresser waiting for someone to come along and open it so she could dance again. Even the yellow and white rose covered bedspread remained on her bed. She remembered how Maddie had made that bedspread the matching curtains for her sixteenth birthday. They were exact copies of ones Kallie had circled with a red marker in an expensive catalogue but could never afford. The curtains still hung graciously over the old-fashioned extra-long windows.

Kallie remembered the first time she had walked into the house. The feeling of having a bed to herself had been strange at first. At the shack, there had been three of them in one twin bed. Sleeping through the entire night was not something she had been able to do before coming to Maddie's. It had always seemed inevitable that one of her siblings would wet the bed leaving Kallie to change the sheets in the middle of the night. Connie would have and had before, beaten whoever wet the bed, so Kallie became a pro at taking care of it herself without her mother ever being the wiser.

"Doing okay in here?"

Kallie looked back toward the doorway. "Oh yes. I'm fine. There's just a lot to do here, isn't there? I think we should start by trying to find any personal documents, important looking paperwork, that sort of thing."

"Sure thing. Point me in the right direction and I'll see what I can dig up." Amy offered.

Kallie directed her to a wall of built-in drawers in Maddie's bedroom. She had always kept bills and stationery in the deep wooden drawers. It was as good a place to start as any.

Kallie decided to tackle the old-fashioned roll top desk downstairs in the dining room. Inside, she saw a box of "Whitman's Sampler" chocolates. She remembered that box! She smiled at the thought of Maddie keeping it for all those years. She had given the chocolates to Maddie for Christmas, somewhere around the time she landed her first job as a teenager. She opened the box and saw a stack of letters tied together with a single piece of red yarn, tied in a bow.

The envelopes were addressed to Maddie but not one of them had a return address. She wondered who they were from but felt uncomfortable reading them. She knew they must be personal and important also since Maddie kept them tied together in a safe place.

She knew they weren't meant for her to read but unfortunately, reading them was going to be the only way to determine whether they were something she should keep or toss out. She would open just one envelope to figure out its importance or lack of.

Kallie carefully opened the first letter and skipped directly to the bottom of the page looking for a signature. Her hands began to shake as she scanned the letter and saw the name, *Connie Jansen* scrawled at the bottom. The letter was signed by her mother? Why, of all people, had *she* sent letters to Maddie? The childlike writing on the page fueled the anger and outrage Kallie was quickly having a tough time containing. The more she read, the angrier she became. Turns out that Connie had been extorting money from

Madeline for years! In exchange, she would allow her daughter to remain with Maddie. Connie was demanding payment? What was going on? Why would Maddie give Connie money? It was Connie who hadn't wanted to be her mother anymore!

As she read on, Kallie began to see the big picture a whole lot clearer. Rifling through the letters, each demanding more cash than the last, she felt sickened by the ruthless woman that had given birth to her. She had abandoned her own ten-year-old child on a bench outside of a store and never looked back. Yet she had the nerve to extort the kind, thoughtful woman who took her in. She knew very well that Maddie cared about Kallie and would do anything to save her from being a ward of the state or worse yet, taken back to her abusive mother. The letters were many and didn't stop until the month Kallie left for college.

A ledger in the drawer showed every single payment made to Connie. At first, she had been satisfied with forty dollars each month. Over time, Maddie ended up paying her seventy- five dollars a month to leave Kallie alone. She could feel the rage building up inside of her. How dare that conniving, horrible woman bilk Maddie for her hard-earned money! She worked so hard for every dime she ever had and ended up giving too much of it to a woman who hadn't worked a single day in her entire life!

The very last letter in the box looked different than the others. That one was addressed to Connie and written in Maddie's handwriting. In big red letters at the top of the page was the word "DUPLICATE." As Kallie read the letter, she smiled as the tears streamed down her face.

"Ms. Jansen, the child has left for college. She no longer resides with me. There is no reason for you to contact me ever again. I will not be sending any more money and you do not need to write or call for any reason. I will no longer accept any form of contact from you

going forward. Should you not adhere to my request, I will have no choice but to involve the law."

CHAPTER SIXTEEN

Kallie woke up the next morning feeling more rested than she had in days. Even months. She didn't see Amy or Adam when she walked into the kitchen but noticed a pot of freshly brewed coffee on the counter. She helped herself to a cup and went to the large bay window seat in the living room. Through the window, she spotted Adam outside. He was holding an ax high into the air and letting it fall with smashing force into a piece of wood. Kallie made her way onto the front porch.

"Good morning, Adam!"

He stopped the ax in midair when he saw her and smiled. "Hey stranger! How are you feeling? I'm sorry I haven't had a chance to visit with you much since you've been here. Unfortunately, work is well…work." he laughed.

"No worries! I am so grateful that you and Amy have invited me to stay here with you. Your home is beautiful! What a spot to have all to yourselves."

"Thank you! We like it. We're so glad you're comfortable here. We certainly want you to be. Give me a minute to finish here and I'll come grab a coffee and sit with you for a bit. Amy ran into town to pick up a few things."

"Oh, I don't want to take you away from what you were doing."

Adam chuckled. "Oh, trust me, it's almost time for a break. I've been at it for a few hours now and the sun is getting a bit warmer than I like for splitting wood. I welcome a break and a chance to chat with you for a few minutes."

Kallie sat in the chair on the front porch and closed her eyes as she tilted her head to the sun. The location of the cabin was pure heaven. A private haven away from the rest of the world. From where she sat, it was impossible to know there was a world going on outside of the peaceful spot she was fortunate enough to be enjoying.

Adam continued to drive the heavy axe into chunks. The loud sounds of wood ripping apart gave her a flash of DeJa'Vu, though she couldn't quite put her finger on why. Something about being surrounded by trees and the sound of the wood splitting apart felt strangely familiar. She shook her head and dismissed whatever it was she couldn't seem to form a picture of in her mind. When Adam finished, he made a cup of coffee and joined Kallie.

"So how are you feeling? Not just physically, I mean. You and Amy have both been through a lot in the past few days. I'd imagine finding out that you are sisters was quite a shock to you both!"

"That's for sure! You know, you can't make this kind of crazy stuff up! Only when our mother is involved is *anything* apt to happen!" she laughed.

"I know that Amy has had a tough time through the years dealing with the damage Connie has done. I can only imagine that you have also. Amy shared with me how Connie left you on your own when you were ten? I'm so sorry you had to go through that, Kallie."

"Thank you. Fortunately, Madeline O'Brien was there to rescue me from whatever hell I could have lived if she hadn't come along. I'm so sorry also for the issues that Amy had to deal with. She had to live there with Connie for her entire life. In some ways, I got the better end of the deal. A gift in disguise."

Adam shook his head. "It's good that you can look at such a terrible experience in a good light. You could have gone through life feeling bitter and angry. You and Amy both could have. But you didn't. A couple of tough women, I'd say."

"Amy is an absolute true gift in my life, Adam. Never again will I be without her. I never even knew how much I missed being a big sister until now. She has a huge, warm heart and I'm so glad she has you in her life."

He smiled. "Well, she's a pretty terrific woman and it is I who am the fortunate one."

Amy's car pulled up the gravel driveway. She was thrilled to see that her sister and her husband were having an opportunity to visit. Adam's work schedule had been crazy as of late, but she had wanted nothing more than for the two of them to get to know one another while Kallie was still in Maine.

"Well hello to my two favorite people!" she said as she got out of the car. "Someone's been to the farmers market in town! We shall feast tonight my dearies!"

Adam laughed as he descended the steps to carry her loot. "Did you buy out the entire market?"

"Laugh now! Enjoy all the fruits of the farmers hard work later my dear! I found the most beautiful ears of corn that we can cook on the grill for dinner. Oh, and the potatoes and tomatoes and…well you'll see all my treasures soon enough."

Adam leaned down to kiss her as he stood with both hands full of vegetables. Kallie smiled watching the two of them. They were so in love and genuinely happy, that was obvious to anyone who saw them together. Coming from the life she and Amy had, it made her heart dance to see that Amy had found a kind of love like she had also found with Cam. Both sisters had been blessed with healthy, happy marriages unlike the one they saw as children.

"I'll take the bags in, hon, why don't you grab a coffee and sit with your sister while I put things away." he offered?

"You are the best!" she said as she kissed him once more.

"I can't tell you how happy it makes me to see you happy, Amy. I always wished for this kind of peace for you. For all my sisters. Nice to see that you have found it."

"He's a good man. I feel truly fortunate to have his heart."

Adam rejoined them on the porch after a brief time. He brought with him a fresh pot of coffee and pretended to be a waiter as he served the sisters. He dripped coffee down the side of Amy's mug and onto the porch floor as he poured her a fresh cup.

Amy laughed, "You better stick to your day gig babe."

"I think you're right there my dear. So, ladies, tell me, how did two women grow up with the likes of Connie Jansen and turn out to be such beautiful people?"

Amy and Kallie laughed in unison. Kallie asked, "I take it you have been unfortunate enough to meet her?"
"Well, meet would seem like a friendly encounter, which it was not. I am aware of who she is since I've been called to the property more than once, while on duty."

Kallie smiled. "Now that does not surprise me in the least. Let me guess, she was drunk and doing something she shouldn't have been?"

Adam nodded. "She was drunk all right. She and another of your sisters, Brandy, tend to get drunk and call the police on one another regularly it seems."

"That's sad. Amy was telling me that Brandy turned out just like Connie. I wish that hadn't been the case. Amy, what about Ginger?"

Amy had hoped they could talk more in depth about their siblings and their lives as children. She was glad to see that Kallie felt up to the conversation now.

"Ginger is doing well. She graduated high school and married a man named Ben Harris. He used to deliver for a local beverage company. After they were married, they moved to Massachusetts. She gave Connie a piece of her mind before she left and vowed to never see her again. She hasn't been back to Maine since. When Adam and I eloped, Ginger and Ben were there with us. We keep saying we are going to get together one of these days, but life just keeps us both so busy. She sells real estate and Ben went into insurance sales, so they are always on the go."

Kallie felt a tear run down her cheek. "I'm so glad to hear this, Amy. It looks like both of you did so well considering the odds you had stacked against you."

Amy reached for Kallie's hand. "You also had those same odds my dear sister. You also did very well."

"I would love to meet Ginger at some point if that's something she would be up for."

Amy laughed. "Oh, I'm sure she would. She's a peach, Kallie. You will love her. We'll have to work on planning something for the three of us!"

"I'd love that! I have been thinking and I've decided that I'm going to see Connie while I'm here."

Amy's eyes grew wide. "Why on earth would you want to do that?"

"For starters, I'm not going to let her get away with the fact that she kept us all apart. Finding out that she knew exactly where I was that time and never told any of you about me, tears me up inside. Also, I need to know why she dropped me off and left me for dead in the first place. I mean, who does that? Why would any mother do that?"

Amy looked at Adam with concern. "Kallie, I know you have plenty of reasons to want to give her a piece of your mind, but I don't think any good will come from a run in with Connie. The woman is pure poison. Trust me when I tell you that she only got worse with age!"

"I've thought about that and figured as much. Still, she owes me some answers."

Amy nodded. "I couldn't agree with you more, Kallie but you have to do remember that this is Connie we're talking about. She doesn't think she owes anyone, anything. To think that she will be willing to see you or give you any explanation, is kind of wishful thinking. If there's nothing in it for her, she doesn't do it. That's how she is, remember?"

"Well, if I have to, I'll make it worth her while. At this point in my life, I don't care what it costs me. I need answers and I'm willing to give her whatever it takes to get them."

Adam spoke up. "I know this isn't any of my business, but I'm going to give my opinion anyway. Connie Jansen is a dangerous woman. We don't get called out there because she's a model citizen. She and Brandy beat on each other regularly and when they aren't taking their anger out on each other, they seem to have no trouble finding some unsuspecting soul to direct it at. I think you are being a bit naive if you think she will willingly help you find the answers you need."

Amy interrupted. "And you have just had a terrible accident that you need to recoup from! The last thing you need is either of them ganging up on you! I agree with Adam. You definitely shouldn't go out there!"

"I love you both for worrying about me. I do. But, for me, this is something I am going to have to do. I'd prefer that one of you drive me out there when I'm ready, but if you don't feel comfortable with that, I understand. I can wait until I am able to drive again. Please understand it's something I need to do. I've spent my whole life without answers as to why I was tossed out. Now, I need them more than ever."

Adam grinned. "Well, I see that you both have that same stubborn nature about you. If you are anything like your sister here, and I fully suspect you are, then your mind has already made up. When you feel well enough, I will drive you out to the shack."

Amy didn't like the idea at all. "Kallie, isn't your life back home a good one? Why do you care what Connie has to say? Does it really matter, all these years later, what reason she had for leaving you? She's the last person you should be concerned with at this point I would think."

Kallie loved it that Amy was worried about her safety both mentally and physically. Still, it was something she knew she had to do. She had given it plenty of thought over the years and after reading the letters Connie had written to Maddie, Kallie knew in her gut it was something she was going to do, one way or another.

"I am happy at home, Amy. I have a wonderful husband who loves me and supports me. I have a wonderful career and I love what I do. Still, deep inside, I've spent my entire life feeling this need to prove that I was good enough. Even as a young girl, I felt like I wasn't good enough. I felt that I didn't really fit in anywhere. Even when something good happened, I was always waiting for the other shoe to drop. I always felt like someone was going to find out that I was Connie's daughter, and I would be exposed for the low life that I really was. I know it sounds ridiculous now, but that's how I felt. I got good, the older I grew, at being a chameleon. I knew what people wanted me to be, expected me to be, and I became that. Cam was the first person in my life to know all about Connie and the life I had with her. Fortunately, the man is amazing and has stood by me through the years, no matter what."

"See! Life is good for you, sis, why go mucking around in the garbage that Connie will most certainly dish out?"

"I've come to realize that a person cannot have a future without first dealing with their past. I just need to know why. She's the only one who can fill in those blanks for me and then I can move on. Please understand, Amy. It would mean so much to me to have your support in this."

Amy had tears running down her cheeks. "My heart breaks for you! Knowing you felt that way your entire life kills me. You never, ever deserved to feel that way. I hate it that she did that to you. To all of us. I wish you wouldn't go, but I understand that you have to."

"Thank you, Amy. Your support means the world to me."

Amy added, "Honey, as much as I appreciate you offering to bring Kallie to see our "mother, it should be me who takes her. Although, I need to tell you, Kallie, that I can't see her with you. I will bring you there and wait in the car. I can't bring myself to re-open that can of worms. I shut that door a long time ago and for me, it will remain closed. I hope you understand?"

Kallie more than understood. Amy had dealt with their demon mother, in the way that she had, years ago. It was Kallie's time to confront her. Just knowing that her sister understood, was more than enough. Kallie stood to embrace her sister and once again, they purged their hearts of the years of hidden pain that had been buried deep inside. With each tear that fell their hearts felt just a bit lighter.

"Well ladies. I say we husk that corn and get our feast ready! Does anyone want to join me in the kitchen? There may be a nice glass of wine in it for you!"

The remainder of the evening was one that Kallie would always remember. Laughter filled the evening air as the three of them enjoyed the meal of delicious fresh vegetables on the grill as well as Maine lobster and clams. The instant bond she had with Amy was more than she could have ever hoped for. She would cherish this time with her sister for the rest of her life.

As she crawled into bed that evening, Kallie knew the day was coming when she would be strong enough to return to that shack in the woods. It would be one of the hardest things she'd ever have to do but she knew it wasn't an option. She also knew that no matter what happened, no matter what she may encounter with Connie, Amy would be there for her and would help her handle it. However it was that she'd managed to live her life without her sister, didn't seem to matter anymore. Kallie knew that never again would they let anything come between them. There would be nothing that Connie or anyone could do that could break the strong bond of sisterhood they had found.

CHAPTER SEVENTEEN

The following week went by fast for Kallie. She continued with the physical therapy sessions and felt good about the progress she made each time. The external bruises were fading to a translucent color all over her body. From time to time, she still felt sharp pains under ribs, but they were becoming less and less painful each day.

As promised, Amy helped her with the preparations for Maddie's service. Without her assistance, Kallie wasn't sure it was something she could have pulled off on her own. Organizing and running around town to pick things up wasn't as easy as she'd first thought. She could have done more if not for the heavy cast on her leg slowing her down. Thankfully, her baby sister stepped in to make sure things ran smoothly.

The funeral home was gracious enough to offer a room in the back for people to gather and have light refreshments. Amy made sure they were well stocked with coffee and baked goods from Russell and Doris' kitchen. Kallie wasn't sure what she would have done without her little sister.

She was glad to see so many people from town, as well as from the surrounding towns, pay their respects to Maddie. Kallie always knew how giving and caring she was, but she truly had no idea just how many folks Maddie had helped through the years. The stories of kindness that had been given freely by Maddie, made her smile. She had truly left her mark on this world and then some. Kallie had lived long enough to know that this is not something that can be said of many people.

She spent her days with Amy at the cabin when they weren't traveling to the hospital or cleaning out Maddie's house. Amy knew of a homeless shelter in Bradford that gladly accepted the household items they were donating. Kallie knew Maddie was smiling down on them as they dropped box after box off to folks who had nothing. Even though the week was a whirlwind of activity, Kallie was enjoying the time she spent getting to know Amy better. As it turned out, Amy was a fantastic cook. This was something Kallie did not have in common with her sister. The excitement Amy had for mastering a new dish was infectious. Kallie did her best to assist in whatever task she could from a stool in the kitchen. Usually, she assumed the role of the sous chef and was fine with that. She could peel potatoes or carrots with the best of them. Anything beyond that, she didn't really excel at or have a desire to master. It was a good thing that Cam enjoyed cooking, or they would have eaten a whole lot more takeout dinner.

The ability to relax was also something that Kallie didn't share with her sister. Before coming to the cabin with limited mobility, she wasn't remotely accustomed to taking time to relax. For as long as she could remember, she was a textbook overachiever. But life at the cabin was different than her life back home. There, she was learning how to simply enjoy the moment she was in.

Cam called her every day. Sometimes three or four times a day, depending on what his schedule looked like in London. He was jumping at the bit to get the deal done and get back home to his wife. They had discussed him coming directly to Maine when he returned, and Kallie was looking forward to the possibility. She wanted him to get to know Amy and Adam as she was having the opportunity to do.

She didn't once mention to Cam about her plans to see Connie. She knew there was no way he would be in support of that idea! It was best if he didn't know until afterward, she decided. It took everything he had to stay in London after her accident, but he would throw the entire deal out the window if he'd known about her plans to confront her mother. She would tell him when the time was right, which would be after the fact.

Kallie had spoken to Amy earlier in the day about the idea of going to see Connie, soon. Her sister voiced her opinion about it once again but maintained that she would take her when she was ready. Kallie was ready. She'd waited a long time to stand face to face with the woman who left her to find her own way in the world at ten years old. She'd had plenty of time since coming to the cabin to think about what she would say. Still, she had no idea what she would say until she was in the moment. After therapy the following day, Amy had begrudgingly agreed to take her out to the shack.

+++++++++++

The undeveloped land along the familiar old gravel roads had remained unchanged since Kallie was a child. There were miles and miles of nothing but trees and an occasional barn or shack here and there. As Amy drove, Kallie thought about all the times she'd dreaded riding that stretch of road on the school bus. She always wished the bus route would one day be different and the driver would take her somewhere else, anywhere else, but home. They passed the brook that Kallie remembered bathing in from time to time when there was no running water at the shack. There was absolute silence as they rode. Amy wasn't particularly happy about Kallie going, so she'd thought it best to say nothing at all. In her mind, Kallie weighed all the reasons she needed to go versus all the second thoughts she was having.

Amy broke the silence. "Are you absolutely sure you are up for this? I can just as easily drive on by, you know. You do NOT have to do this!"

Kallie shot her a reassuring look. "I'm sure. I'll be fine, Amy. It's something I have to do. In my gut I know I need to do it. I need answers. Besides, I'm not a child anymore. She has no power over me anymore. Please don't worry. I can handle myself.

I love you for caring, but really, I'll be okay."

Amy pulled the car into the shoulder of the road. A turn off had formed over the years into a makeshift parking spot.

"I will be right here. If you need anything, text 911 to my cell and I'll be in. I'll also get Adam over here too!"

Kallie laughed. "Okay. You sure you aren't the big sister?"

"Ha-ha! Seriously though, please be careful!"

"I promise I will. I'll see you in a bit."

Kallie headed into the path into the woods. It was hard to believe there was a place in there where people lived, but there was. As she continued down the path, she came upon what she used to refer to as "appliance mountain." Every washing machine, refrigerator, television, and stove they had ever used went to the "mountain" after it stopped working. She noted how the pile had grown since she was a child. She wasn't a bit surprised though. That's what people like Connie did with things they no longer wanted. Tossed them out. She had certainly proven to Kallie, years ago, that appliances weren't the only things she got rid of when she was finished with them.

Kallie couldn't help but notice the stillness of the woods around her. Where were the songbirds that she'd become used to hearing at Amy's cabin? There was nothing but a deafening silence all around her. She wondered if Connie managed to find a way to frighten even the wildlife away.

"You know you're in hell, when even the birds don't dare to fly around!" she whispered aloud.

As she approached the shack, she was amazed at how much more it had deteriorated since she had last seen it. Kallie never thought it possible to be in worse shape because it was grossly run down back then. A piece of metal from an old STOP sign was nailed to the door over the spot where glass had once been. She took a deep breath as she stood in front of the door. She raised her hand to the splintered door, but the door flew open before her hand hit it. Kallie reached for a makeshift rail to catch herself as she almost fell backward.

A rough, haggard woman stood in the doorway obviously annoyed. Her chestnut brown hair, dyed a shade too dark, piled high on top of her head in an old-fashioned beehive style. Clumps of dried orange foundation, caked on much too thick, cracked with her facial expressions. She wore a mint green polyester pantsuit and sparkling gold plastic high heeled sandals to finished off her white trash ensemble.

Kallie was speechless. She wasn't sure what she had been expecting Connie to look like but this wasn't it.

The woman was clearly irritated. "Yah? What?" she bellowed.

Kallie opened her mouth to speak but looking at this woman had thrown her of guard. She didn't even know where to start. She had a thousand different responses spinning around in her head but couldn't seem to grasp a single one.

"I SAID what the hell ya want? If ya sellin' somethin,' I ain't buyin'!"

The woman leaned against the door frame with one hand and the other on her hip. Her long, yellowed nails painted a light pink showed the inches of dirt that had collected beneath them.

A sinister grin spread across the woman's face. "Kahlua? That you Kahlua? It is ain't it?! Little miss snooty pants finally come home to roost, has she?"

"Excuse me?"

"Excuse *you*?" she laughed. "Kahlua Delicious has done come on home to Mama!"

Kallie instantly felt the sting of the word "Mama" She hadn't referred to Connie as "Mama" in a very long time and she wasn't about to start now. She may have given birth to her but that was all she could lay claim to. Connie cackled revealing a row of blackened top teeth and nothing but gums where the bottom teeth had once been.

"Hello Connie."

"Oh, it's Connie now, is it? Don't ya mean Ma?" she laughed like she had heard a joke that only she had been privy to. "Ain't this somethin'! Ain't seen hide or hair of ya in well over twenty years and now here ya are on my porch! Get to the point, girl. What THE HELL do ya want?"

Kallie shifted her weight from her cast. "I don't want anything. I just came to talk. That's it."

Connie scowled. "That right? Well, I can't imagine what ya could possibly want to talk to me for!"

"I've got some questions I'd appreciate answers to. That's all I'm asking for. Just a little of your time. That's it."

"Oh sure. Let me just put *my* life on hold so I can do anythin' and everythin' I can do help you out!" she continued laughing. "You are funny girl. You always did think you deserved some special treatment! I can see right now that nothin's changed."

Kallie rolled her eyes. Somehow, she doubted Connie's social calendar was remotely filled. The crusty old woman was enjoying herself as she toyed with her. That was more than apparent. "I'm not sure what's so funny. I just want to have a simple conversation with you. That's all."

"Oh, I heard ya. I ain't deaf. Don't have to keep repeatin' ya'self! Oh boy! Wait 'til Brandy gets a load of this!"

"Brandy? Is she here?" Kallie felt her heart begin to race in anticipation of meeting her for the first time since they were children.

"Duh! Where else ya think she'd be? She ain't gonna be none too happy to see ya neither!"

"What? Why not? Why wouldn't she be happy to see me?"

"Geeze. I can't imagine! Why would anyone not wanna see Miss Queen Bee herself?"

The mocking tone was beginning to get on Kallie's nerves. She couldn't imagine why her sister would be angry that she had come to talk. She hadn't seen Brandy since she left all those years ago. She hadn't seen any of them since that time.

"Ya gonna just stand out there lookin' like a dumb ass or ya comin' in?" she demanded.

Kallie reluctantly followed her inside into a room she recognized as the kitchen. It still had the same dark, dinginess to it. And there was no mistaking the strong odor of mold that she had forgotten through the years. A makeshift table leaned against the wall with two wooden chairs pushed up to it. The table consisted of an old Formica tabletop with stacked milk crates as legs. The chairs didn't look all that stable either. She gingerly sat down in one of them hoping not to fall. Beside her on the floor, a rusted silver bucket filled with fermenting rotten food, made her stomach turn. The old -fashioned hand pump still sat on the countertop, even though it had never worked.

As Kallie looked around, she could see that not much had changed in her absence. Nothing had changed for the *better* that was for certain. Doors were still without knobs; large chunks of linoleum were missing from the floor. Patches of wallpaper were still missing from the walls. At the back end of the kitchen, there was a doorway that had once led to the living room. A wool gray blanket, riddled with moth holes, hung from the frame as a makeshift door. From behind it, emerged a woman that Kallie assumed could only be Brandy. As a child, she had the wildest bright, orange-red hair. As an adult, that hadn't changed a bit. If not for that, Kallie may not have recognized her at all.

Brandy was about five feet tall and must have weighed well

over two hundred pounds. If she hadn't known better, she would have guessed Brandy to be many years older than herself rather than younger. She hadn't aged well at all. Her skin was the consistency of well-worn shoe leather. Sadly, she had obviously taken her wardrobe advice from Connie. She wore a green and black checkered flannel shirt and a pair of tight black jeans with holes throughout. This was a look Kallie had seen often on Connie. Though it was hard to make out the little girl she had once been, she knew it was Brandy.

Connie was the first to speak. "Hey Brandy! Look what the cat done drug in! This here's ya big sista, Kahlua!"

Brandy snapped her head quickly in Kallie's direction. "What? Ya gotta be kiddin' me! You mean to say that my big sis, the one and only Princess, the one who thinks she is so much better than anybody else, has done dropped in for coffee?"

"Hello Brandy!" Kallie offered.

Brandy slowly walked toward her in a defensive, unfriendly manner. Kallie felt her entire body stiffen. Brandy moved in face to face with Kallie. So close that Kallie could smell the unmistakable odor of alcohol and onions. With squinted eyes, Brandy kept turning her head like she was trying to figure out if what she was seeing was real.

Her voice boisterous and much too loud. "Well, I'll be darned! Looky here! If it ain't THE ONE AND ONLY KAHLUA JANSEN! RIGHT HERE IN THE FLESH! Ya sure got some nerve showin' ya face around here!"

What was she talking about? What were either of them talking about? *She* was the one abandoned and left to fend for herself and those two were acting like she had done something wrong to them. Kallie looked at them both, trying to find a single grain of similarity between herself and them. They were all related, as much as she hated to admit it, but the similarities stopped there. She looked nothing like them. She acted nothing like them. She felt nothing for them.

Kallie thought of how she and Brandy were inseparable as children. They were more like best friends and not just sisters. Being the two oldest girls, they protected each other and their younger siblings, from Connie, as best as they could. They had never once had an argument. Whatever Brandy was talking about...whatever she was mad at her about, made no sense to Kallie at all.

Connie stood in the kitchen pleased as punch. "She ain't said what she's wantin,' 'cept to talk."

"Talk? Why the hell ya wanna talk to us? I can't stand the sight of ya so don't be expectin' me to sit here and talk to ya 'bout nothin'! We ain't friends Kahlua! Hell, we ain't even family. If that's what you thought, then you sure as hell are dead wrong! I ain't got nothin' to say to ya."

Confused as to why her sister was acting this way toward her, Kallie questioned, "Brandy, I don't understand where any of this is coming from. I really don't. All I wanted was to come here and get some things sorted out in my mind. I don't know why *you* are so angry with me or what I could have done to you to make you feel this way about me."

Brandy laughed. "Oh please! Poor lil Kahlua don't ever do nothin' wrong, does she? What? We supposed to feel sorry for *YOU*? Well, if that's whatcha came for, it ain't gonna happen, I can tell ya that right now!"

Connie moved away from the sink where she had been leaning. She went to the refrigerator, which must have been circa 1975. There was more duct tape on it than enamel. Kallie heard the old familiar sound of a beer cracking open. "Ah, hell, I ain't got time for this. Spit out whatcha want so ya can get the hell out!"

Brandy shook her head and closed her eyes. "Ma! If you wanna talk ya can but I ain't tellin' her squat! I'm goin' back to bed. Wake me up when she's gone then you can take me down to Oscars."

Oscars was the dive bar in town. The only bar in town. Kallie was surprised it was still open. Somerfield's finest drunks frequented often, including Connie. And evidently Brandy too.

"Wait, Brandy! I'd really like to know why you are so mad at me." Kallie pleaded.

"Oh, for Christ's sake Kahlua, why should I be mad? All ya done was run off and leave me here to take care of everythin' on my own. While ya went and lived the high life with some rich ole lady. Nah, I can't 'magine what my problem with YOU is!"

"Brandy, I didn't run off and leave you. I had no choice. MOTHER took me into town that day and left me there. She told me to find a new life, a new home, and a new mother! Brandy, I swear!"

She didn't believe a word Kallie said. "You're a damned liar! Ya think 'cause you lived a good life and got outta here that you're smarter than me now? I might look stupid to you, Kahlua, but I ain't!"

"Brandy, I swear to you that I'm telling you the truth. Tell her Connie! Tell her how you took me to town and abandoned me all those years ago! Tell her what you did to me!"

Connie sipped her beer and grinned. She didn't say a word. She was enjoying the banter between her daughters. That much was evident. Brandy looked as old as Connie as she glared at her sister. Life with Connie could do that to a person. Finally, her mother spoke up. "Ah hell don't make no difference now anyhow. That was a friggin' long time ago! I ain't sorry I done it neither. Could be it was the smartest thing I ever done!"

Brandy didn't say a word as she sat down at the table and lit a cigarette. She poured herself a Rum and cola and drank half of it in one gulp. Kallie's heart felt heavy seeing Brandy like that. She wished she were seeing something entirely different as she looked at her sister. Again, she attempted to explain to Brandy what she had been through. "Is that what she told you? That I ran away and was living with rich people? That I never looked back because I thought I was better than you all? Brandy, I lived in the next town over, in Bradford. An older woman there raised me after our mother dropped me off in town and told me she was done with me."

Brandy took another gulp of her drink and muttered, "Whatever."

Connie was smiling now. "Well, there ya go! If ya got what ya came for...don't let the door hit ya on the way out!"

"It's about time you told the truth, Connie! I can't believe you held onto that lie for all these years. Well, I can believe it. Nothing should surprise me about you by now! I have some questions for you and maybe you could also see fit to tell *me* the truth?"

"Oh really? Turns out I'd like a lot of things too, but I don't see what I want droppin' from the sky!"

Kallie ignored her and looked directly at Brandy, "Remember when we were kids? And she and Daddy would drink too much and get to arguing? Then all hell would break loose, and they'd start throwing things at each other's heads and anybody else who was in the way? Remember the beatings we took Brandy? You must remember how we had to run out of the house, day, or night when they were crazy drunk and got it in their heads to start beating on us for no reason? Don't you remember the cartwheels in the dark? Sometimes it was the middle of the night when we were outside hiding from them for hours until the house got quiet again and was safe enough for us to go back in? Don't you remember me teaching you all how to do cartwheels like I had learned at school, just to pass the time until it was safe to go back inside?"

Brandy rolled her eyes and went to the cupboard. Kallie was surprised when she brought her a glass and poured her a drink. "Rum and cola if ya want it!" she grumbled and slid the glass toward her sister. "Yah? So, what if I remember. That was a long time ago. What's that got to do with anythin'?"

"I was just thinking about it that's all. I've been thinking about a lot of things from that time in our lives."

Connie piped up, "What THE ACTUAL hell Brandy? She comes in here talkin' bad about your Ma and you gonna sit there at MY table and share ya booze with her now? I'll tell ya one thing right now. I ain't sayin' nothin' about nothin' for free! Anybody wants to know anythin' from me they better be havin' cash IN HAND!"

Kallie wasn't surprised. "Oh, it's so comforting to see that some things never change Connie."

She snorted, "That right? Well, from where I'm standin' don't look like much changed with you neither! Once a piece a garbage, always a piece a garbage. And ya know what else? Just for that, I decided I ain't tellin' you nothin.' Time ya get on ya way now Fancy Pants. I seen all the likes of ya I care to see for another twenty years if that soon."

Brandy didn't say another word. She stood up and walked back behind the gray blanket. Connie stood holding the door open and motioning for Kallie to go through it. That was it. Not one single question answered. When Connie was done with something, she was done. Kallie knew that all too well.

She stood on the step and turned back to Connie. "I want to know why, Connie! Why did you leave me there on that bench that day?"

Connie took a final drag off her cigarette before tossing it out the door in Kallie's direction. Before she had time to ask again, the door slammed in her face.

She yelled through the door, "Great seeing you both as well. Take care and you can rot in hell, Connie!"

She slowly made her way down the path and back to the car where Amy was waiting for her. She got in the passenger side, took a deep breath, and began to bawl from a place she'd not visited in her soul for many, many years. Amy didn't say a word but put her arm around her sister and let her cry.

CHAPTER EIGHTEEN

The water was coming down hard against her skin. She could barely keep her eyes open against the driving rain. It was pitch dark outside. She quickly looked for shelter, but it was useless. She couldn't see two feet in front of her with the rain and fog clouding her vision. Where was she? Why was she outside in the middle of the night? In the middle of a storm?

"I thought I'd find you here!" came a loud male voice from the darkness.

The deep tone of voice stirred up a fear that she'd known somewhere before. Whoever had spoken to her wasn't visible. Who was that? What did he want? She didn't know why she was afraid, but she knew she was. Every fiber of her being was shaking. Maybe it was from the chilly rain or from pure fear, but her bones were rattling. It didn't really matter which, all she knew was that she was cold, tired, and wanted to be somewhere else.

"Who are you? What do you want with me? Go away!" she yelled.

A deep sinister laughter echoed through the night. "Oh now, you know that's not going to happen. Come over here and get what you have coming to you girl!"

She ran as fast as she could without knowing where she was going. Anywhere far from that voice was all she cared about. She ran until she could run no more. Her bare feet hurting from the sharp branches on the forest floor. She stood behind a tree, hoping to hide from the footsteps that had been following her. She hoped she had outrun whoever it was. As a hand landed on her shoulder from somewhere behind her, she knew she had not. All she could do was scream.

"Kallie? It's Amy! It's okay. Another bad dream is all. You're okay."

Amy cradled her in her arms as Kallie shook. "I don't know what that dream is all about but it's the same dream I keep having, only it gets worse every time!"

"Let me make us some cocoa. We can chat for a bit. I'll be right back okay."

"That sounds good. Thank you. I'm so sorry if I woke you up."

"You didn't. Adam called a few minutes ago to tell me he was working overtime, so I was already awake."

Amy left the room and returned with two mugs of cocoa. She crawled under the covers beside her sister. "What happens in the dream you keep having?"

"I'm always hiding. It's dark and storming outside. Every time there's someone there with me but I can't see who it is. Someone I fear, that's for sure! I just don't know why. I don't know what I'm supposed to be taking from this awful dream. It's like it's trying to tell me something, but I just don't know what. I just want it to stop."

"I can't say I blame you. Doesn't sound like something I'd want to keep revisiting over and over again."

"Nope. Anyway, thanks for the cocoa. You are the best!"

"You're not so bad yourself, sister."

The next morning, Kallie decided it was time to go through the box of paperwork that Amy had collected for her during the first trip to Maddie's house. She still had a lot to do at the house before the realtor came to look at it. It was still very much full of everything Maddie had collected in a lifetime.

Amy took the box of paperwork from the closet and laid it on the floor in front of Kallie's chair.

"It still feels weird to be going through Maddie's personal

things." Kallie said.

Amy nodded. "I would imagine so. But it's something that has to be done, I suppose. Let me know if there's anything I can help with. I'll be in the kitchen. I'm going to try my hand at whipping up a ham, cheese, and broccoli quiche for us. Adam will be sleeping for the rest of the day I would imagine. The poor man never got in until seven this morning. If he's lucky, we mighty save him a piece." She winked as she left the room.

Maddie had kept every bill and every receipt for the bills she'd paid, for years. Kallie was pulling receipts out of the box from twenty years earlier. Fortunately, the night they had brought the box back with them, the life insurance policy she was after, had been right near the top of the stack. Kallie had dropped it off with Attorney Miller, who would be setting up the scholarship fund, as Maddie wanted.

As she looked at each paper, Kallie tried to decide what if anything, was worth keeping. She found birthday cards for Maddie that went well beyond twenty years. She had saved every single one that Kallie had ever given her. Every "thank you" card was also kept, all tied neatly together. The woman kept everything it seemed. Kallie finally decided to keep them but everything else could go. She didn't really know why she should keep the cards, but she just couldn't bring herself to throw them out. She felt like she had made satisfactory progress as she neared the bottom of the cardboard box.

A manila envelope was the very last thing in the box. The words "Do Not Throw Out" written in Maddie's handwriting in red ink. Kallie opened it and almost dropped the coffee mug she was holding in her hand.

"What in the hell?" she said aloud.

Amy walked into the room with a plate of quiche, fresh from the oven, for each of them. "What's up? Find something good?"

Kallie took the plate and set it on the coffee table. "Amy! You are not going to believe THIS!"

Amy sat down and began to read an old, yellowed newspaper clipping that Kallie had found. "What? You have got to be kidding me!" she exclaimed.

"Right? See what I mean! Read it aloud to me, will you? Just in case I read it wrong the first time!"

"Oh, I don't think you read anything wrong but okay. Here goes! The heading of the article reads, "Somerfield Wife Questioned About Disappearance of Husband.""

Connie Jansen, wife of Albert Jansen, was transported to the Somerfield Sheriff's Department for questioning regarding the alleged disappearance of her husband, Mr. Albert Jansen. According to a friend of the family, Lucinda Emerson, Mr. Jansen hasn't been seen or heard from in over a month. She claims that the last time she heard from him, he was going to his home on 37 Runyon Lane in Somerfield. However, Mrs. Jansen disputes this claim saying that she hasn't seen him in months. The two have been separated for quite some time, according to Mrs. Jansen. Anyone having any information regarding the whereabouts of Albert Jansen should call the Somerfield Sheriff's Department at 207-444-3210

"What disappearance? I never even knew he was missing! Did you?" Kallie asked.

Amy shook her head. "No! I had no idea. Like I told you back at the hospital, he was just never there. She told us not to talk about him. Period. So, we didn't. I never had a memory of him anyway, to be honest."

"According to the date on this, you would have only been about a year old. That was somewhere close to the time she dropped me off in town. It had to be. I remember you were about a year old."

"Oh my God, Kallie! Do you think she did something to him?" Amy asked with wide eyes.

"I wouldn't put anything past Connie to be honest, Amy. When I was a kid, he had a habit of taking off and coming back when the welfare check came in the mail. The fact that Lucinda, whoever she is, reported him as missing tells me that he just didn't show up again at some point. Do you know who she is? I can't say I remember ever hearing that name before."

Amy shook her head. "Nope. First time I've ever heard the name. I bet we can look her up online though. See if she's still around here."

Kallie agreed. "Good idea. Let's see what's out there about Ms. Lucinda Emerson! Just because I'm curious as all get out now!"

Amy laughed as she ran for her phone in the kitchen. "Me too. Odd that our mother never wanted us to talk about him don't you think?"

"Truthfully, everything that woman does is odd!"

Amy agreed. "True. Okay so there's a Lucinda Emerson located over in Williamsville. That's got to be her because there are no others listed. Or, she could have gotten married at some point and changed her name, I suppose. Let's see what we can find on social media."

Kallie laughed. "We are creeping on some poor woman we don't even know!"

"True. But she won't know we are. Let's just see what we can find."

"Amy, what if we do find the exact same woman from the article? What do you suggest we do? Interrogate the woman for reporting our father missing?"

"We could see if she'll talk to us. What do we have to lose Kallie? Your Maddie must have felt there was some truth to it, or she wouldn't have kept the article for all these years, right?"

Amy had a point there. Maddie was never one to gossip

about anyone. If she kept the article, there must have been a darned good reason. Otherwise, she would have dismissed it as a rumor. Still, the idea of contacting a woman neither she or her sister had ever heard of and grilling her for information on their father, that neither of them really cared whether he was alive or dead, somehow seemed crazy.

"And what if our father is alive out there somewhere? Do we even care, Amy? I know that sounds awful, but let's face it, I don't think we really do. Am I wrong?"

"You're not wrong but what if he's *not* alive out there somewhere and Connie had something to do with it? And what if we were able to prove she did?"

Kallie laughed. "Okay. That's a lot of "ifs" and get real! We could have caught her in the act of any criminal activity, and she'd lie through her teeth. You think she's going to come right out and say oh yes, I did something to my husband over twenty years ago. I confess!"

"Well, we just have to dig deep enough to prove it without a doubt and then she can't dispute anything." Amy rationalized.

"I think that's a bit of a stretch my dear sister. But hey, I have nothing better to do right now, I'll just sit back and drink my coffee while I watch you go on a wild goose chase."

"Ha! Ha! Don't be so sure it's a wild goose chase. I just found her on social media. I'm going to message this Lucinda Emerson and see if she will talk to me."

"Oh my God! You did not! Seriously? What are you going to say to this woman?"

"I'm going to tell her that I am Albert Jansen's daughter, and I would like to know if she'd like to meet for coffee because I'd like to discuss what happened around his disappearance all those years ago."

"Well good luck. If she's smart, she put Albert far away in

her memory. The man was never good for anything, Amy and I'll bet she doesn't have exactly fond memories of him, if it is the same woman. Which I'd like to note that I highly doubt."

"Doubting Thomas aren't you, Kallie?" Amy teased.

"Okay that's fair. I guess on this particular subject I am. Work your magic sister and see what you can come up with."

"Kallie! Look! She just answered me. I asked if she would be willing to meet with me and my sister over coffee to discuss our father, who we don't know much about. She said, "most certainly." You name the time and place and I'll be there."

"No way! She doesn't even know us! Jesus, Amy, is this even a smart idea?"

"We have nothing to lose at this point. Connie sure as hell isn't going to tell us anything! Let's just see this woman and take the newspaper clipping. We can see what she says and decide if we believe her or not. Please say you'll come with me!"

Kallie thought the entire thing was insane. She knew it was insane. But she wasn't about to let Amy go alone and it was the least she could do for her sister who had done so much for her.

"I want it known that I don't like this idea. At all. But because you've asked me to and I can see this is important to you, I will go. Besides, there's no way I'd let you go alone."

"Thank you! Okay let's tell her we will meet her in Bradford at the diner. When? Maybe tomorrow morning after your physical therapy appointment at Pineview?"

Kallie took a deep breath and rolled her eyes. "Sure. We can do that. I'll try to contain my excitement until then." she laughed.

"Brat! Thank you, Kallie. I know you don't want to and you're just going for my sake. See what I've missed all these years without a big sister to look out for me?"

Kallie reached for her sister and gave her a hug. "And you will never have to know that feeling again."

CHAPTER NINETEEN

As soon as she had finished physical therapy, Amy was waiting for her at the front door of the hospital. Therapy was going well, and there was talk of the cast coming off at the end of the week, which was only two days away. The idea of not having to carry around that extra weight and gaining back her freedom was beyond exciting to Kallie.

"Guess who may get her cast removed on Friday?" she squealed as soon as she got into the car.

"No way! Oh Kallie, that's wonderful news! See! All these sessions have paid off now haven't they! As much as you didn't like the idea of doing them at first, I bet you're glad now that you did!"

"You got that right! I forgot what it feels like to have two feet to walk on instead of one foot and one clunky walking cast. Best news I've had since finding out that you are my baby sister!"

"And who knows we may find out more good news today when we meet this woman." Amy winked.

"Are we still doing that? Are you sure it's a good idea? I mean, what good can come from it? I told you, Connie will never admit to any wrongdoing on her part. Everything that's ever been wrong in her life is someone else's fault. This would be no different. And that's a big IF the woman really knows anything that isn't just gossip!"

Amy shook her head. "Well, that all is true, I know. But I say it's worth our time to at least meet her and see what she has to say."

Kallie laughed. "I know. I know. And that's why I'm going to go with you. It's going to cost you though; my chaperoning services shall not be free young lady. I'll need a coffee and a piece of pie."

Amy grinned. "Deal! I think I can manage that fee."

+++++++++++++++++++++

There were no other customers inside the diner as they chose and sat at a booth. Kallie thought it odd that Amy led her to the exact same booth at the diner, where she had chosen to sit the first time she was there. She wondered how many other things she and Amy did that were similar and had no idea the other one did also.

"So, Ms. Amy, how are we going to know who this woman is?"

"She had a photo of herself online. If it was a recent picture, I think we should be able to figure it out. Also, look around here, Kallie. I don't think it's a typical busy time of day for this place by the look of it since we are the ONLY customers here at the moment!"

Kallie looked around the diner as they broke out into laughter. "Once again you are right my dear sister."

Kallie noticed the way Amy was anxiously ripping open sugar packets for her coffee. She seemed to be getting more anxious as the minutes went by.

"I would have figured she would have been here by now." Amy said.

"Maybe she decided it was a bad idea to have a conversation with someone online and agree to meet them face to face?"

"Well, it's not like I'm some sort of serial killer or something!" Amy snapped.

"Sorry. I shouldn't tease you like that. I know you're not some crazy person but I'm just saying, this woman has no idea that you aren't. Maybe she thought better of the idea?"

Amy shrugged her shoulders and slowly sipped her coffee as she noticed a woman step through the door. It had to be Lucinda Emerson. She had dyed bleach blonde hair about three quarters of the way down her head. The part not dyed was a solid white color. Skinny jeans, way too tight and a top that was much too low for a lunch date at the diner. Even from the distance, it was easy to spot the heavily applied blue eye shadow and thickly applied foundation, a shade or two too dark for her complexion.

"Kallie! That woman who just came in has to be her."

Kallie turned to see the woman who was about sixty years old or so and about her height of five feet six inches. A sparkly silver purse hung from her shoulders with matching dangling silver earrings. Her bad dye job thrown atop of her head in a messy bun.

As the woman approached the table, Amy noted the high heeled silver sparkling sandals that also matched the purse and earrings.

"You Amy?" the woman blurted out when she reached their booth.

"I am. You must be Lucinda. This is my sister, Kallie. Thank you so much for coming."

Lucinda shrugged. "Figured I didn't have anything to lose being a public place and all. Besides, curiosity kept me up all night. I know it killed the cat and all that, but I couldn't stop thinking about what you might want with me. Said you wanna talk about Albert huh?"

"We do. And I'm sure it wasn't easy making the decision to meet two total strangers, but we really appreciate you taking the time to come today, Lucinda."

"Sure. No problem. Anymore coffee in that jug?" she asked as she slid in next to Kallie.

Kallie realized she'd seen this woman recently. She thought sure she recognized her from Maddie's service.

"Excuse me, Lucinda, but did I see you at Madeline O'Brien's service?"

Lucinda snapped her head around to face Kallie. "Yeah, I was there. Why you wanna know?"

"Just curious. I thought you looked familiar. How did you know Madeline?"

Kallie watched the tenseness in Lucinda's shoulders relax. "That woman was something else, I tell ya. Every year at Christmas, she would bring a box of homemade cookies and hand knit mittens to my house. She didn't know me from a hole in the ground, but that didn't matter a bit to that lady."

Kallie smiled. "No one was a stranger to Maddie. Just friends she hadn't yet met, she always used to say."

"So, you knew her too huh?" Lucinda asked.

Kallie nodded. "I did. She was an incredibly special lady with the biggest heart. She will be missed by many."

Lucinda agreed and then looked back at Amy. "So, tell me, what exactly is the reason we are meeting today?"

Amy refilled the mugs and tried to decide where to start. "I don't know where to begin, really."

"What is it ya wanna know about Albert? How do you two know him?"

Amy smiled. "Well, that's a long story really. But he is, was, our father. And how do *you* know him?"

The woman's face went pure white. "You don't say? Both of you? You're both his kids?"

They nodded in unison. Kallie asked, "Did you know him well?"

Lucinda laughed. "Know him well? Well, I'd say I did. For over fifteen years, he and I were together."

Kallie was taken aback. "Together?"

Lucinda explained. "Shocking ain't it? He was with me long before he met your Ma. One night he was running around drinkin' with the boys and next thing I knew this woman, Connie, was at my door talkin' about how she was pregnant with his kid!"

Amy and Kallie had absolutely no idea as to Albert's history with this woman and the surprise was clear on their faces.

"I can see that you both didn't know nothin' about that. So anyway, he left me and married that tramp. But I don't know why. It wasn't like he was ever gonna make an honest woman out of her. I tried to tell him, but he was never one for takin' advice. The man had a skull a foot thick. Stubborn as all hell."

Amy gently pushed for more information. "So, he left you, married Connie and that was that?"

Lucinda slapped her hand on the table. "Huh! Hardly! Shoulda been but I wasn't none too bright back then either. When he wasn't with me, he was with your Ma. I suppose that's how you all came about."

Kallie was confused. "So, you knew he was married to Connie, and you continued to see him?"

"Like I said, I was young and stupid. Thought I loved him and couldn't live without him. At first it made me angry when he didn't turn up back home for days. But I always knew where he was over on the other side of town with your Ma. After a while, it's just how it was. He spent time with both of us. I didn't like it, but I didn't wanna lose him either. I always thought your Ma knew where he was when he wasn't at home with her. Until, well, until I figured out, she never knew we was still together all those years."

Amy asked, "How did you figure out that she had no idea he was still with you?"

"Well, about the time he turned up missin,' I guess. Aw hell, missin' my ass. The woman did somethin' to him that's what happened. I'll go to my grave believin' that. She's guilty of it, I tell you. Nothin' ever gonna be able to convince me otherwise!"

Kallie mentioned the newspaper clipping. "We found a newspaper clipping of an article written about the investigation of Albert's disappearance. That's how we found your name, Lucinda. Can you tell us more about that time?"

"What is it ya wanna know girl? One day he was here. Next, he was gone for good. He went to Connie's like he was always doin' when she got the welfare check. She was dumb enough to let him help her drink it all up and then he always came back to me. Until he didn't come back."

Amy asked, "What made you think she did something to him? Maybe he found another woman somewhere else and just took off from both of you?"

Lucinda cackled. "Nope. You mighta known Albert as your Daddy but I knew him as a man. Ain't no way in hell he was leavin.' He had the best of both worlds. Everythin' he wanted with me plus whatever it was he saw in that tramp. Sorry. No offense."

Kallie chimed in, "No offense taken Ms. Emerson. We are fully aware of the kind of person our mother is. There's nothing you could say about her that we could possibly be offended about."

"Where's that girl gone to? I'd like some hot coffee."

Amy waved the server over and asked for another carafe of coffee before she started asking Lucinda for more information.

"What makes you think Connie did something to Albert?"

"Well, it's simple. That's the only way he wouldn't come back home to me. That and I believe that Connie found about Krystal and her rage done got the best of her!"

Amy and Kallie didn't understand. Amy asked. "I'm sorry, we don't know who Krystal is."

Lucinda shrugged, "Well that don't surprise me much really. Guess there ain't no reason you shoulda known. Krystal is my daughter. Mine and Albert's daughter. Your sister."

You could have heard the world's smallest pin drop after Lucinda's revelation.

It was Kallie who spoke after the awkward silence. "Our sister? You and Albert had children?"

"Just the one. My Krystal was born about a year before Albert turned up missin.' I think your Ma heard about my baby and it was more than she could handle. It was one thing sharing him with me and quite another to know that he had given me a child. She always acted like she was better than me, lordin' a parcel of Albert's kids around. She acted like what he and I shared meant nothing. Like I meant nothin' to him because he hadn't given me a child."

Amy raised her brows. "I don't even know what to say. We have a sister. Another sister. Another sister that we've known nothing about for all these years. Is there no end to the lunacy that is Connie Jansen?"

Kallie reached across the table and put her hand on Amy's. She felt like her entire body was shaking. She had gone a lifetime without knowing she had a big sister in Kallie and now she was learning that she had another sister who was about her age.

"Please understand, Ms. Emerson, that we just learned about one another recently. It's a long story. A super long story for another time. Connie kept us from knowing one another and now we find out that she has kept us from knowing your daughter, our sister, as well. It's kind of a lot to take in."

Lucinda nodded in agreement. "I'm sure it is. I'm sorry to be the one to have to tell you about Krystal. Your Ma shoulda been the one but I guess since she didn't tell ya about each other, there was no way she was gonna tell ya about my child."

Amy's hand shook as she lifted the cup of coffee. "Seriously! Are there anymore siblings out there we know nothing about? This is absolute insanity!"

Neither Kallie nor Lucinda responded but instead stared into their coffee mugs. Kallie felt the same way Amy did but she knew it was important for her baby sister to get out her frustration. Hers could wait.

Amy continued with her outrage. "I mean, c'mon, who but Connie's kids have these kinds of ridiculous issues to deal with? Don't most people know who their own siblings are? That aside, what happened to Albert? Does anyone know for certain?"

Lucinda answered, "No one knows for sure, Amy. But I'm tellin' ya, my gut says she did something to him. There is no way on earth he was ever going anywhere else. Why would he?"

"So, you're saying that you truly believe Connie did something, as in killed him and that's why he hasn't turned up in all these years?"

Lucinda nodded. "I know it sounds crazy but believe me, I know that woman is over the top nuts and jealous as all hell."

"I'm confused. You're saying that my mother knew about you for years? Knew about you and her husband continuing to see one another? Knew that when he wasn't with his family, he was with you? If she were going to do something to him, why wouldn't she have done it when she realized he was running around with you?"

Lucinda tried to explain. "Because it was one thing for him to be coming over to the house and staying with me, when they'd been arguing or when the money was gone. It was quite another for him to give me a child. It was like she had some privilege over me that wasn't mine to have. Ever. When that was no longer the case, I believe with all my heart, she lost her freakin' mind."

Kallie didn't know what to believe. "Okay, I know firsthand how insane this woman is. I'll be the first to agree that she is downright nuts. But killing her husband kind of nuts? And hiding it for over twenty years? I don't know. Sounds over the top even for her."

Lucinda disagreed. "Listen girls. I went to see her when Albert didn't show up like he always did. Like I said, after the first of the month, he was always back at my door. Facing her was something I didn't want to do but I had a bad feeling in the pit of my stomach that just wouldn't quit. When I asked her where he was, she told me that he had run off with someone younger. I knew that wasn't true. I could tell she was hiding something the way she smirked at me the whole time I was standing in her yard."

Kallie asked, "So that's why you went to the police, and they ended up questioning her about his disappearance?"

"Actually, no. I waited a few more weeks and I knocked on her door again. She was nastier and meaner than the time before. She told me about how he never loved me and was out looking for someone who didn't look so haggard. Well, I had to remind her that if it were true, that he'd left her for the same reason too!"

Kallie's eyes grew wide, "I'm sure she didn't like that much. Connie, as I recall, never did like anyone else being able to throw jabs in her direction. She was the only one with an opinion and it was always the right opinion!"

"Oh no! She didn't like it none, but I said it anyway. As I was turning to leave that day, she yelled out my name. So, I turned around to see what she wanted. She had the evilest grin on her face and said "wherever he is, he's gone, and he's gone for good. He ain't never comin' back to you or anyone for that matter." and then she shut the door and I never talked to her again. That is when I decided to go to the cops."

Amy asked, "And they never found anything out as to where he was one way or another?"

Lucinda was picking at the peeling neon pink nail polish on her thumb nail. "Nope. They said it was probable that he had run off with some young woman. Said they had no reason to believe otherwise."

Kallie was amazed. "So that was that? They just took her word for it and stopped looking?"

She found herself wondering why she even cared where Albert Jansen was. She didn't really. She was there at the diner, meeting with this real-life cartoon character, for her sister Amy's sake. The longer she sat and listened, the more she hated the idea of Connie getting away with yet another demented thing. She believed in her heart that Connie was capable of anything. Kallie also wondered what good it did, all these years later to give it an ounce of thought space in her head. If Connie had done something to her husband, she had obviously gotten away with it. What was worrying about it now going to do?

"You know," Amy said, "the thing here is that I never even knew my father. I don't have a single memory of him, and I bet even if I had known him, I would despise him as much as I do Connie. I'm sorry Lucinda, if that offends you, I don't mean to do that. It's just that he sounds like the same crazy loser that my mother is, and I wouldn't have cared for him either. Still, I can't help but feel myself getting angry at the idea of Connie getting away with something like that all this time. I mean if she did. And let's face it ladies, she probably did."

CHAPTER TWENTY

Adam could see the flames from the stone fire pit as soon as he pulled into the driveway. Amy and Kallie sat around the fire bundled up in blankets drinking wine. Seeing them there, together, laughing and enjoying each other's company made him smile. Finding Kallie was the best thing that had happened to Amy in a long time. He could see with his own eyes, the way she floated around the room as though she didn't have a care in the world. She had found a part of her herself that she never realized she was missing, and he was happy for her.

"And what do we have here ladies? A party that I wasn't invited to?"

Amy leaned toward him for a kiss. "Well, actually, yes! We had something of an unusual day to say the least. We figured it was a great evening for a fire and an endless supply of wine."

Both sisters giggled as they faced one another and agreed.

"I see. Let me change out of my uniform and you can tell me all about it. I'll bring my own beer." he smiled as he walked off.

The girls went back to their conversation. "Kallie! Do you remember Fridays at the shack? How every Friday morning, Connie would get up, throw her hair up in rollers, as though she had some prominent place she had to be? Shave her legs, pluck the already too thin eyebrows and gob on handfuls of makeup?"

Kallie was laughing so hard that she could barely speak. "Oh, do I ever! She'd run around all morning until late afternoon in that torn and tattered old, quilted cheap bathrobe like she was royalty or something!"

"Oh yes! I had almost forgotten about that robe! Pink with

gold satin around the edges! Fitting attire for a frigging shack in the middle of the woods!"

Kallie was holding onto her stomach that ached from laughing so hard. "All that primping just to go to Oscars Bar where the men there didn't know what soap and water was!"

Amy about fell out of her chair. "Oh, she had some doozies through the years from that place, let me tell you!"

Adam smiled as he approached the two of them laughing hysterically. "Okay, fill me in, what'd I miss?"

Kallie spoke up, "You didn't miss anything much. Just our fondest memories of our mother!"

Amy started giggling even before Kallie had finished. Adam didn't remember a time that he'd seen her laugh so hard. It was nice to see her happy. He knew she'd been happy with her life before meeting Kallie, but this was a happy that only a sibling could bring about.

"Oh, I see. You two actually have fond memories of life with her?"

Kallie laughed as she tried to get the words out. "No! That's exactly it! We don't have a single actual memory that we can call a happy one, do we sis?"

Amy was laughing so hard she had tears streaming down her face. She wiped them with the sleeve of her sweatshirt.

"Oh my God no! Plenty of memories, but good ones they are NOT!"

"So, this must be a sister thing? I don't know what you two are laughing so hard about. Nice to see you both happy though!"

Kallie tried to explain. "See, Adam, that's just it..." and she lost her composure again. Amy was right behind her with the roaring laughter.

"How much wine have you two had?" he asked.

Amy grinned, "Not enough!"

When they had finished the last bottle of wine, Adam helped them both to the cabin. They were hungry for breakfast food and Adam made them eggs and hash browns before making sure they made it to bed in one piece.

When Amy awoke the next morning, Kallie wasn't up yet. Adam would sleep until early afternoon in preparation of his night shift later in the day. She brewed a pot of coffee and took a cup with her to the pond. She'd gone to the pond often through the years to think. Adam had stocked the pond with trout years before and every now and then she'd see the ripple on top of the water as one broke through the surface to grab an insect. There was something rejuvenating about the pond and the wildlife she'd often seen around it.

She sat on the ground, cross legged with her coffee and stared at the glassy surface of the water. Sometimes it felt like she had her own giant crystal ball as she peered into the motionless clear water.

Memories of the night before with her sister made her smile. Never in her life did she think she could love someone she had just met, as much as she loved Kallie. Apart from Adam, of course. For as long as she lived, she would be forever grateful to the Universe for bringing them together. And at the opposite end of the spectrum, Amy would be forever unforgiving of Connie for keeping them apart.

Revisiting the conversation with Lucinda the day before, made her blood begin to boil again. She was determined that she would not let Connie get away with one more thing. She had spent a lifetime getting away with every terrible thing she'd ever done and there was plenty of terrible things. Connie was one of those conniving people who always changed the story just enough to shed the light of blame on someone else. No matter what she'd ever done, she took zero responsibility for it.

Abandoning Kallie and not giving a second thought as to her safety and welfare was unforgivable. Keeping her from her siblings was also unforgivable. Amy knew in her heart that she didn't really care one way or another if Albert Jansen was alive or dead. But she did care if it was at the hand of his wife that he had gone missing. If she'd had something to do with his disappearance, Amy wanted her to pay for it. In her heart and mind, she felt it was high time that Connie pays for something she'd done. One way or another, Amy knew she was going to find the proof she needed that would show Connie's guilt. It was time for "her feet to be held to the fire" for at least one wrongdoing in her lifetime of wreaking havoc.

Amy had no idea where she would begin to find the proof she needed, but in time it would come to her, and she would act on it. That much she knew for certain. She didn't care if it took her the rest of her life, she was going to find the answers she needed to nail her mother for what she'd done.

CHAPTER TWENTY-ONE

Kallie laid in bed listening to the birds sing outside the window. She had spoken with Cam late into the night, as he was on London time and was finally back at the hotel after a day of meetings. Kallie had intended to get to bed early and get a good night's sleep, but the bottles of wine she and Amy finished off the night before changed that plan. Besides, she'd been too excited to sleep. She would be losing the extra weight on her leg later in the day and she couldn't wait! She was glad that Cam had called to take her mind of things. He was thrilled to hear that the cast would soon be off. He had less than a week left in London and was anxious to hold his wife in his arms again. It had been a long time since he had held her and so much had happened while they were apart. He'd promised her no work for at least two weeks when he got back home. She would have every second of his time to do whatever she wanted. Kallie had been through a lot since the last time she laid eyes on her husband. There was a lot of catching up to do. In more than one way.

Every time she did close her eyes throughout the night, intending to sleep, she recalled the conversation with Lucinda Emerson at the diner. Kallie believed, like Amy, that Connie had done something to Albert. What she worried about more than either of her parents was how the entire thing was affecting Amy. She understood why her sister felt the need to force Connie to have a consequence for her actions, just once in her life. But not at the risk of Amy becoming consumed with retribution. She had lived long enough to understand that revenge is a tricky thing. It can start out with every intention of doing the right thing but sometimes, somewhere along the way, it can turn on a person and totally consume them. She didn't want that to happen to her sister.

Amy had been through enough having lived a life with their mother. One that she got to escape from, at least partially. If there was a way to undo the past and free her sisters from a life with their mother, she would. But there wasn't. There was only this drive to nail Connie to the wall that was consuming Amy. And scaring Kallie.

The bedroom door burst wide open as she lay deep in thought.
"Good morning sleepy head! Do you know what today is by any chance?" Amy squealed.

"Hmmm…. let's see…is today the day we win the lottery? Or maybe it's the day we go on a trip?" she laughed. "Of course, I know what day it is silly girl! I couldn't sleep a wink last night! I've been so ready to see this ugly ole thing disappear from my leg!"

Amy sat on the edge of the bed. "I can't even imagine how uncomfortable that's been for you! I'm so glad today you will be free!"

Kallie nodded. "Me too!"

"Let's go into Waterport for lunch afterward and maybe do a little shopping?" Amy suggested.

"That sounds like the best plan I've heard in ages! Let's do it! But on one condition."

"Uh oh. Sounds ominous. Okay, what's the condition?"

Kallie smiled. "You have to let me treat you to lunch! I have no way to repay you and Adam for what you've done for me, so at least let me buy lunch! I've got this beautiful platinum card that I haven't been able to use in weeks! It's burning a hole in my pocket as they say! Deal?"

"Okay. I'll let you buy me lunch. Just so long as it's not too expensive." she grinned.

They both laughed. Amy relented. "Well, let's just see how

the day goes."

Two hours later, they were at Pineview where Kallie was anxiously awaiting to hear her the nurse call her name. An hour later and the girls were on their way to Waterport minus the heavy leg cast Kallie had started the day with. Waterport was significantly larger than both Somerfield and Bradford and was the closest thing to a city in the area. There were boutique shops and an assortment of small eclectic restaurants to choose from.

Kallie felt like a new woman. "Oh, before lunch let's stop there!" she squealed as she pointed to Thomas Jewelers. "I love looking at jewelry! You up for that sis?"

Amy agreed. "Up for it? You just try and keep me out of that place!"

"I take it you've been here before?"

"Hahaha! Oh yes! A time or two. I about drove Adam crazy when picking out our wedding rings. I can't tell you how many trips we made to this store. By the time I had decided on exactly what I wanted, the entire staff greeted me by name when I came through the door!"

Kallie smiled. "Hey! A girl knows what she wants when she sees it."

The older woman behind the counter greeted Amy by name. Amy laughed and shot Kallie an "I told you!" wink.

Kallie wandered down the wall of long glass display cases hoping to find just the thing that would catch her eye. She stopped when she found it. A dainty white gold charm bracelet with a charm that read "sisters" on it. She asked the clerk to wrap five of the bracelets for her while Amy was still chatting with another clerk, gushing over the anniversary bands she hoped to receive one day.

Kallie had been thinking of something she could get for Amy to show appreciation for all that she'd done to help her since the day they met. As soon as she saw the bracelet, she knew she needed five of them. It was a long shot to think that Brandy would be interested in sharing a bond with her, or with any of the girls, but she would attempt to give her one anyway when the time was right. Then there was Ginger, who may or may not be receptive to an intimate piece of jewelry from a sister she had never met. And, of course, there was Krystal, who hadn't ever met *any* of the Jansen girls. Regardless of whether they would want them, Kallie was going to purchase them and hoped that there would be an appropriate time to give them all one before she went back to Virginia. If not, she considered mailing them along with a letter to each of them.

She would give Amy's to her as soon as it was boxed and paid for. At the moment, her sister was busy trying on rings at the far end of the store. Armed with a pile of boxes, Kallie interrupted to give Amy the gift. The clerk looked a little relieved for the intrusion. When Amy opened her gift, Kallie thought she should have waited until they were in the car. Amy's melt down at the jewelry counter attracted a lot of looks from the other customers. She had plenty of tears.

Oh, Kallie! You don't know how much this means to me! I will cherish this forever, I swear!"

Kallie hugged her tight and told her that she loved her. "I'm so glad you are my sister, Amy. I've been without a sister for so long and you will never know what you mean to me!"

"Likewise, sister!"

"I also got one for each of our sisters, including Krystal. Maybe at some point, before I go home to Virginia, we can see them all. If not, I'll mail them and include a letter to each of them."

"I don't know how we have all lived without you in our lives, Kallie. I really don't! You are a wonderful, caring, generous woman and I'm so proud to call you my sister!"

"Right back at you, Amy. Now that we've taken up these kind folks time with our therapy session, how about we go grab some lunch."

Amy drove to the Brick Oven Deli, which was one of her favorite places to eat. They sat at a pub table in front of a wall of windows overlooking a river gorge below. The smell of freshly baked bread was intoxicating. Suddenly they both realized how hungry they were.

A server brought menus highlighting organic offerings, most of which had been locally grown. Amy knew exactly what she was going to order and suggested that Kallie try it as well. The chicken pesto with sprouts sandwich on fresh baked bread was the best Kallie had ever had anywhere. She could see why Amy loved the cozy bistro style deli.

As they sipped the Chai Tea after lunch, Kallie realized that it was the first time she'd ever had a sister to go for lunch with. It felt good to feel a connection in her soul with someone who shared the same DNA.

"So, Ms. Amy. Anymore thoughts on how we could proof that Connie did something to her darling Albert?"

"No. I've been racking my brain over it but like you said, she's not going to just offer up a confession to me. Or anybody for that matter. I don't know *how* but there has to be a way!"

"I've been thinking too. I don't want you to obsess over Connie and give her anymore of the space in your head than you already have. She's so not worth stressing over and I know you know that. Maybe we should just let it go? Let her go on with her miserable life?"

Amy was shaking her head. "Nope. Absolutely not. I promise you I won't let her ruin my life or make me into some obsessive, crazed lunatic but one way or another, if it's the last thing I do in this life, I will watch her get arrested and see her finally pay for something that she's done. I'm sick and tired of always watching her get away with everything. You know what she did to you was wrong. What she did to all of us was wrong. And she didn't bat an eyelash about any of it."

"She doesn't feel bad because she has no conscience and no soul, Amy. That's my point here. You do have those things. Despite her, you have become a wonderful, caring, giving person. Carrying around so much hatred for someone is bound to change a person after a while. I don't want that for you. I suspect that's partly what's to blame for Connie being the way she is."

"I know what you're saying, Kallie. I do. Please believe me when I tell you that I won't change. I won't become like her. I'm just so tired of seeing her always fall into a pile of garbage and come out smelling like roses. It's not right!"

"No, it isn't. But look at your life and then compare it to hers. I'd say you've already won. Wouldn't you?"

Amy knew that Kallie was right, but she wasn't ready to let Connie scrape by one more time. Maybe someday she would be willing to let the entire thing go. But not today.

"Okay sis, you win. How about no more talk or thoughts of her today? Do you want to shop some more while we're here or are you ready to head back to the cabin?"

"As much as I can't believe I'm going to say this, I think I'll pass on the shopping for today. I didn't sleep much at all last night because I was so excited to lose the cast today. And we got up early and it's been a beautiful day with you, Amy. It really has. I think I may be up for an early evening if you don't mind?"

Amy laughed. "Oh, thank goodness! I was hoping you were going to say that! I didn't sleep last night either. An early night would be wonderful! I think Adam will be working a double shift tonight to cover for a co-workers vacation. It would be a good night to hit the hay early and catch up on some sleep."

Amy admired her bracelet on the drive back to Somerfield,

which made Kallie's heart warm. She hoped that the other girls would feel the same. Even if they didn't, she felt good about giving the gift to them. What they did with it afterward was up to them. Kallie had come to Maine not having a relationship with any of her siblings. Since being back in Maine, she'd found out that her nurse was her sister and learned of another one that none of them knew about. She knew the trip to Maine wouldn't be one that was going to be easy on her, but she'd had absolutely no way of realizing what a long, strange trip it would be.

When they returned to the cabin, Amy realized that she didn't have to help Kallie down the hall to her room any longer.

"Hey! You can get around all on your own this time, can't you!"

Kallie laughed and sang, "I'm a big girl now! I can do it!"

"Ha! Ha! You kill me! Your sense of humor is so awesome girl!"

They were both exhausted and in their beds by nine p.m. Kallie wasn't long for this world and fell asleep about the time her head hit the pillow. It wasn't long after that when the hauntingly familiar dream came for her again.

She was hiding behind the giant maple she had hidden behind so many times before. The tree was her favorite hiding place because it was large enough to hide behind and no one would see her there. She realized she had seen that same tree over and over in her dreams.

She could see an outline of the woodshed through the mist and fog. A dull yellowish light spilled out from inside. Someone was in the woodshed. In the middle of the night? She felt a sense of Deja' vu. She'd been here before. She felt her heart racing faster and faster. Suddenly she was aware that she was outside, in the dark, in her nightgown and bare feet but didn't know why. Why was she hiding? What was she doing out there in the dark? Who was in that woodshed? It sounded like someone was throwing things around inside the shed. Like they were looking for something as they tossed aside every-

thing in the way.

A sense of fear came over her. Why was she afraid? She'd seen this all play out somewhere before. She felt she should know what was going to happen by now. But she didn't.

The creaking of the shed door opening startled her. Someone stepped outside with what looked like a shovel in hand. Who was that? What were they doing in the middle of the night in the wood-shed rifling around for a shovel?

Panic began to creep through her body. She suddenly became aware that she wasn't supposed to be seeing what she was seeing, and the pounding of her heart made that clear. She was supposed to be in bed, sleeping. She should have been. She wished she was at that moment.

The person with the shovel was standing still, looking down at the ground. There was something there in front of that person but what was it? Just then a patch of fog floated away making clear to her what was on the ground. There was a person laying on the ground. Not moving. No one was moving. Someone was standing over that person and looking down at the body for the longest time with no movement.

A night owl screeched, and the shovel dropped to the ground. Whoever it was, looked directly toward her. Had she been seen? She was terrified that she had. She was shaking like a leaf as she stood as still as she could and looked directly into the eyes of her mother. As soon as Connie looked away and began to drag the body away from the shed, Kallie made a run for it. She ran as fast as she could for the shack and back to the bed that she should have never left in the first place. She ran as fast as she could and never looked back. Once under the covers, she heard footsteps coming closer to the bedroom window. She held her breath as though that would somehow help. She realized she had witnessed something she never should have. She knew she could never let on that she had seen a thing. Never could she tell an-other living soul about what she'd seen.

Kallie sat bolt upright in bed soaking wet with sweat. That was it! That was the dream she'd kept having except it wasn't a dream at all! It was real. She had seen Connie in the woodshed looking for a shovel that night so long ago. She'd seen her standing over a body that lay motionless on the ground. No, there was no dream about it. Her mind had been trying to get her to remember a scene she'd witnessed so many years before. A memory that was important to recall. The jigsaw puzzle memories were sliding into place now. Things were finally beginning to make sense and Kallie knew what she needed to do.

CHAPTER TWENTY-TWO

Oscars Bar looked just as it had when Kallie was a kid. She remembered waiting outside the rundown building often while her mother went inside for a drink. Connie was always going to be right out after a "quick" drink, which usually lasted for hours. Kallie recalled sitting against the brick wall outside the front door waiting for her mother to come out and trying not to make eye contact with the creepy drunks that walked past. "I see this place is still a shit hole!" she muttered as she turned the key to the off position. Just as she had so many years earlier, she waited for her mother to stumble out the door. It was after eleven p.m. on a Friday night. She was sure Connie was inside. She highly doubted the woman had changed her habits through the years. After an hour of watching a parade of drunks filter in and out of the bar, she decided she was done waiting. She wasn't a child anymore. She could walk right in the front door.

As she swung open the filthy glass front door, she was smacked in the face by a thick cloud of stale cigarette smoke with tinges of cigar smoke mixed in. The place was darker than she'd imagined it to be when she was a kid though she shouldn't have been surprised. It took a minute for her eyes to adjust to the room without windows and bad lighting. As soon as they did, she spotted Connie in the back of the bar. She was sitting at a table drinking with some man Kallie hadn't seen before. Her mother sure found some real winners through the years in that bar. Connie's "date" had a wild, long gray beard and dark, beady eyes that barely shown from under his ratty ball cap. There had to be twenty empty shot glasses lined up on their table. Kallie marched toward the back, in their direction. Her mother's "date" spotted her first.

"Well, well, what do we have here?" She noticed the drip of drool laced with chewing tobacco slide from the corners of his mouth as he smiled.

Connie turned to see who he was talking about "Aww hell! You again? What ya doin' stalkin' me or sumthin? That's 'gainst the law ya know!" They both cackled as though she had said something hilarious.

Kallie wasn't laughing. "Go ahead and laugh old woman. Laugh all you like. The joke's on you this time!" she smirked. Kallie had never in her life felt more empowered than she did at that moment. "You may want to excuse us, Mister! Your date and I have some things to talk about."

"He ain't goin' no-wheres! You can get lost but he ain't goin' no-where's!" she sputtered.

Kallie took a roll of bills from the front pocket of her jeans. She flipped through the wad of bills until she found a one-hundred-dollar bill. She slammed the money onto the table in front of the drunk. If she knew her mother's men like she thought she did, he would take the money and he would be gone. Sure enough, he scooped up the cash, got up without saying a word and left the bar.

Kallie took his seat after he had practically run from the bar. "Hmm...I guess he wasn't all that into you after all Mummy dear. Let's you and I have us a little chat, shall we?"

Connie wrinkled her forehead and snarled, "Ain't got nuthin' to say to ya! Told ya that back at the house. You *are* still as dumb as a rock ain't ya?"

"Go ahead and call me all the names you want. Say whatever hateful, rotten, mean things you can think of. I'd expect nothing less from you! What you don't understand is that things are a little different now than they were back at your house. I'm not a child anymore. I don't take orders from you and your pathetic words of hate can't hurt me anymore. YOU can't hurt me anymore. That must really make you angry, doesn't it?"

Connie cracked another beer and shrugged her shoulders.

"Let's talk about when I was a kid why don't we? Where should we start? Hmmm, Oh I know, let's go back to when I was oh let's say about ten? You remember that don't you? No? Well, let me help you refresh your drunken memory."

"I dunno what the hell ya talkin' 'bout girl. Can't a person have a drink and a little peace and quiet" she yelled aloud to a mostly empty bar.

The smirk on her face told Kallie it wasn't going to be an easy thing to do, dragging the truth from the old bat. She was in no hurry. She had all night, and she would wait all night if that's what it took. One way or another she was going to hear her mother say the words she needed to hear. "No? You don't know what I'm talking about? Let me tell you a little story. You like those don't you? I assume that since you have spent a lifetime making up lies, you'd appreciate a good tale.

Once there was this innocent little girl who trusted and believed in her mother. Yes, I did say she *trusted* her mother. Even though she knew in her heart she had not one single reason to do so. Still, being her mother and all, she *wanted* to trust her. Sure, she should have known better, but she was just a kid. Just a kid Connie."

"Oh, for Christ Sake, enough already. If I gotta listen to this garbage, I'm gonna need a beer. Maybe a few. I'm also gonna need somethin' a whole lot stronger if ya expect me to sit here and listen to ya make up some stupid story. Why don't ya take that wad of cash back out and buy me a drink. You ramble and I'll drink. If not, I ain't got the time."

After Kallie ordered Connie a couple of beers and an entire bottle of the cheapest rum on hand, she continued. "Let's see, where was I? Oh yes, I remember now. Once there was this little girl. Hmmm let's call her Kallie, just for fun. Her mother told her to get into the car one day. And she's a good little girl so she does as she's told. She rides all the way to the center of town with her Mama where the car stops, and her Mama tells her to get out of the car and go sit on a bench. Oh wait! I almost forgot the suitcase. Yes, the little girl's mother had packed a suitcase for her child and shoved it into her little hands just before she got into her car and drove away. Yes, Connie, can you even imagine? The mother drove away and left her small little child right there in the middle of town all alone. She even tells her to find a new mama and to never come back home. Tragic, isn't it? Well, that's not the half of it! You see, that little girl didn't understand why her mother didn't want her anymore. As she sat on that bench and waited for her mother to come back, she tried as hard as she could to figure out why her mother didn't want her anymore. Well, as it was getting dark and she was scared, she started to cry. Can't blame the kid. She was just a little girl! Fortunately, a wonderful woman came along and took her into her home and raised her as her own. Wasn't that nice of that woman to do, Connie? Why, I can't imagine what would have happened to that little girl if she hadn't. Can you?

Agitated and taken aback that Kallie was giving details of something she obviously didn't want to discuss, Connie spoke. "Don't know whatcha gettin' at girl but get at it will ya? Not sure why ya think I need a stupid play by play of your little fantasy story!"

Kallie laughed aloud. "Bullshit huh? Well, the problem MOTHER, is that I remember now. I remember it *all.* It took me a lot of years to remember but it sure is crystal clear now. I was there that night, Connie. That night you hoped I would forget forever. The night I saw you in the woodshed with that shovel. The night I saw you standing over that body."

Connie started coughing and choking on her drink. "That's some fairy tale ya go goin' there! Where the hell ya get a story like that?"

"It's not a fairy tale and you know it, old woman. Tonight, it finally all fit together. All of the bits and pieces of memories and dreams I've been having for years all make sense now."

Connie took a swig of beer and never took her eyes off Kallie. "A dream? You're accusing me of somethin' ya saw in a dream? Well, ain't that just somethin'! Seeings its YOU, I can't say I'm surprised!"

Kallie laughed. "The dream just filled in the blanks that I already knew to be true but had forgotten for a very long time. Since I was ten. Seeing you outside the woodshed with a shovel in your hand, standing over a dead body wasn't a dream. You know it and I know it. All these years you let your children, the ones you didn't toss away like common household garbage, believe that their father left them. Fed them lies that he must have walked right off and left them with only you to raise them."

"What the hell do you know about what I did or didn't do after you wasn't around no more anyway? You dream about that too?" she cackled.

"Laugh all you want old woman. You won't be the one doing the laughing for long. I don't know *how* it happened, but I *know* it happened. That night in the fog, I was there. I didn't see you do it, but I know you did something to my father and then used that shovel to bury him."

Connie's face was suddenly white. "Albert? That's what this is all about? Oh hell, he ran off with some young girl he met in town! Everybody knows that! Better come up with a better story than that before you go makin' an ass of yourself any more than ya already have!"

"I know all about that story too. He didn't run off with any girl from town any more than I just left your house to find a better family. You, mother dearest, were behind both of those things and we both know it. I know all about the police asking you questions regarding his disappearance. I know all about Lucinda too."

Connie slammed the beer bottle in her hand down onto the table. She leaned closer across the table. "Don't you ever say that name to me again! You hear me?! You sure as hell won't like what happens if ya do!"

Kallie leaned back in her seat. "I see I've touched on a nerve there. Not a fan of Ms. Emerson huh?"

"The tramp is a lyin' piece of garbage. She's the one sent those cops nosin' around my place to begin with. I told her what I told them. She couldn't stand it that he didn't want her anymore and ran off to trade her in for a younger version!"

"Do you really think she or the police believed that made up story? Have you told yourself that lie for so long that you actually believe it yourself?"

"Don't sit there lookin' all like the cat that ate the canary. You don't know what you're talkin' about, girl."

"Don't I? I sure seem to be getting under your skin about something I don't know anything about. Besides, now it makes sense why you left me on that bench that day. All these years of therapy trying to figure it out and finally I have the answer. You *knew* I was out there that night, didn't you? You saw me running off back to the house and knew you would have to get rid of me because you couldn't risk me telling anybody what I saw."

"This more of your made-up dream stuff, Kahlua?"

"I bet you wish it were, don't you? I have to hand it to you, Connie. You've managed to keep a very dark secret for an long time. Did it ever get to you? You know, the guilt? The guilt of driving off while your child sat all alone on a bench trying to figure out where she would go when the darkness of night came? Did it ever bother you that you let your daughters think I didn't exist? Or that their father just up and left them? Not that he was ever worth a plug nickel, but that's not really the point now, is it?"

Connie shrugged. "I wish I knew what the hell the point is 'cause I'm gettin' real damned sick of listenin' to ya ramble on!"

"My POINT is that you killed Albert. Then buried him the ground somewhere on your property. Then you threw me out to protect your secret. Just in case I was indeed out there that night."

"And why would I do those things? Huh? If you're as smart as you think you is, tell me that. Why in the hell would I do any of it? If I did?"

"Well first off, you did. You did everything I've just accused you of and you know all too well that it's all true. The why is the part I couldn't grasp until I figured it out recently. So, here's what I believed happened. It was one thing to know that Albert had another woman in town. You didn't mind sharing him with her because you knew he'd always be back. Every month he'd waltz back in about the time the welfare check arrived in your mailbox. And that warped arrangement was okay with you. Until you found out about Krystal. Oh, and then everything changed, didn't it?"

"You shut the hell up, girl. I'm done listening to ya story of lies!"

Kallie smirked. "Oh, I bet you wish they were a bunch of lies, don't you? But we both know it's true. All of it's true. It must have been fun for you to make Lucinda feel like she was less than you somehow, because she didn't have children with Albert. Once she did, you must have snapped and lost your mind! Are you really going to sit there and tell me I'm wrong? Because if you are, I don't think you need to bother doing that because you and I both know I'm not wrong."

Connie reached across the table and wiped all the empty bottles from the table sending them flying onto the floor with a crash. Kallie backed her chair away from the table to avoid the shattering glass bottles.

"You listen to me girl and ya listen good! I'm gonna say this once and only once ya hear me?! That miserable son of a bitch came back to me drunk as always. Had the nerve to go on and on about how nice his day had been. Dumb hick spent the day with his baby girl, Krystal, on her first birthday. Number one: I didn't even know about no kid named Krystal. Number two: I had a baby in the shack who was that age too. Ya think he gave a rats ass about her? Think he spent time with her on her birthday? No! But he has a brat with that tramp Lucinda and all the sudden she's a princess that he cares about? No, I don't think so! Ain't no way in hell he was gonna be totin' some bastard child 'round town when he didn't even do nothin' for me or his other kids!"

Kallie was listening intently, smiling, and feeling pure satisfaction. "I see."

"Oh really? Do you really see? That's friggin' funny! Don't think ya gonna sit there and tell me somethin' ya don't know a friggin' thing about! Unless you're sayin' you know what it's like to share a man with another woman? Ya know what it's like to listen to him go on and on about a brat kid he made with another woman? When don't he do a thing for the ones, he made with you? No! I don't think you see at all! Ya wanna know what happened to that useless excuse of a husband? Fine! Nobody's gonna believe ya if ya told 'em anyway! You're right about one thing. I guarantee ya ain't nobody gonna stumble across his miserable body, I can tell ya that right now!"

"Oh, I already knew I was right, Connie. What I want to know is how it happened on that day. I mean, how did you decide that was the day you were going to kill off the father of your children? Just an idea that popped into your head or had you given it some thought?"

"You wanna know about him? Fine! I'll tell ya! You kids was to bed. He comes out the house over to where I was havin' a beer and course, he couldn't just leave me the hell alone. He starts talkin' about that brat again. Says she looks more like him than any one of my kids does. I stood, looked him right in the eyes and smacked him 'cross the face just as hard as I could. That should shut him up but course he was drunk as usual and didn't have the brains God gave a snake."

"Oh, I see. You were mad at him because he didn't care about any of the kids he had with you? Ironic since you didn't care about us either."

Connie snapped at her. "Go ahead and run ya mouth girl. You're the one wantin' to know the truth and I'm givin' it to ya. If you don't wanna hear it, then fine by me. If you do, keep your trap shut and listen for a change!"

Kallie wanted to get up and walk out the door, but she knew that she was going to be held captive by Connie for as long as she wanted her to be, if she was going to hear what really happened that night.

"I apologize. Please go on."

A look of smugness grew across Connie's face. "Yeah, I thought so! So, it wasn't bad enough I had to hear about that kid of his with that tramp. No. Even after I smacked him good, he wouldn't keep his stupid, friggin' mouth shut. Told me I could hit him all he wanted but it wasn't gonna change nothing. Said he loved that woman and that screaming, brat kid too. Said he was leavin' me with all his kids to go be with the tramp. Said he came to understand she was his one true love. Let me tell ya, I seen red about that time! I wasn't thinkin' straight I know that.

"And that's when you did it? That's when you killed him?"

Connie sat back in her chair suddenly aware of what she had almost let spill from her lips. With her back against the wooden chair, she looked at Kallie through squinted eyes. "Killed him? What the hell are you talkin' 'bout girl? Who said anythin' about killin' anybody? You read too many mystery books I'd say!"

Kallie realized that she shouldn't have interrupted and let her finish what she was about to say. "Oh, come on, Connie! Isn't that what you were about to tell me? That you picked up that shovel and smacked him with it? Was it the only way to stop him from leaving you?"

Connie picked up the rum bottle, took a long haul of it and slammed it on the table. "I'd say I'm 'bout done with your lil visit. Past time for you to get headin' down the road! Way past time!"

Kallie laughed. "I'm not going anywhere, MOTHER. Hell, I'm just getting started. I haven't even begun to tell you about the proof I have that you killed Albert. Nope. I bet you don't want to miss that part, now do you?"

Connie tilted her head from the left to the right as though she was sizing Kallie up for a fight. "Ha! That's funny! Proof huh? What did ya dream 'bout some proof too? You is full of it! IF you had proof, you wouldn't be sittin' here askin' me what happened. Knowing you, the trouble makin' little snot that you always was, you'd have been to the cops already. No. I'd say proofs the one thing you ain't got. And if you ain't leavin,' then I am. Sick of lookin' at your face and listenin' to ya high and mightiness DAUGHTER of mine."

Kallie raised her eyebrows. "Spoken like a guilty woman! I notice you didn't deny killing Albert. Do you think I don't have proof? That's fine. Just remember, it's your blood running through these veins of mine, old woman! You haven't known me for a good many years! You don't know what I'd do or what I wouldn't do. Don't sit there being all smug with me. Perhaps I'll just hold onto this proof of mine until I figure it's just the right time to use it against you. Oh, and don't call me daughter. Ever. Again. I am NOT your daughter. I know you can't understand this, but it takes a hell of a lot more work to raise a child than to just bring it into the world and let it raise itself! I am thankful every day for Madeline O'Brien! Without her I would never have known what a real mother is supposed to be. I sure as hell didn't learn that from you!

Connie laughed aloud. "Is this where I'm supposed to say my feelin's is hurt 'cause Queenie don't like her *Mommy* no more? Well guess what? I don't give a damn! Never did truth be known."

"Oh, the truth *was* known. You never gave a rats ass about any of your kids. We were only a means to collect a welfare check that supplied you with booze."

Connie didn't disagree as she titled her head to the side and grinned. "Sounds 'bout right."

"You and I both know you are a sad excuse for a human being. To say I hate you isn't a strong enough statement. If I could find the right words to describe how badly I despise you, I would string a nice long sentence together. I'm not sure there are enough words in the English language to accurately form a sentence to say how I feel about you. You disgust me beyond words. You are going straight to hell, Connie. I have zero doubts about that. Anyone who would raise her children like you did, deserves a special seat right next to the devil himself!"

Connie threw her head back and laughed. "I'll be his best gal. No doubt 'bout it!"

Kallie pushed her chair away from the table. "Thanks for your time, I'm sure you had a million other things you could have been doing instead. Oh wait! This is what you do every day isn't it?"

Kallie walked to the bar and dropped a fifty-dollar bill on the counter to cover Connie's tab, which she knew was more than she deserved. But the satisfaction Kallie got from rattling her cage, was worth every dime and more. As she headed for the door, she yelled back over her shoulder, "Your tab is paid old woman! Consider it a goodbye, good riddance and go to hell present!"

CHAPTER TWENTY-THREE

Kallie sat in Amy's car wondering what she should do next. She was a little agitated with herself for interrupting Connie at the very moment she felt an admission of guilt was about to fly out of her mouth. If she had been just a little more patient and not cut her off, she may have been able to get a confession from her. The audio recorder on her cell had been on the entire time, under the table, and she could have had something that resembled a guilty admission. The look of rage on Connie's face as she talked about Albert and Lucinda, was all the admission that Kallie needed. But she realized she needed real, physical, concrete proof if she was ever going to be able to get any law enforcement agency to listen to her.

As she sat in Amy's car, she replayed the conversation over and over in her mind. Out of the corner of her eye, she spotted Connie, practically running from the bar, and climbing into an old clunker of a truck. Kallie smiled and whispered aloud, "Well, well. Didn't take her long to run out of there now did it. Wonder what the odds are that she's not going to make sure her little secret is still safe?"

Kallie grinned as she thought about her mother panicking at the idea of her having proof that she committed murder and that she could use it against her anytime she pleased. Just in case she was right, she decided to follow her home. If she was indeed checking to see that her crime had not been discovered, Kallie hoped to catch her in the act.

"Sounds easy enough. The guilty always go back to the scene of the crime in the movies. Connie's dumb enough to do that and when she does, I'll have my phone recording her on video!"

Kallie took the phone from her pocket and smiled as she put the car into drive and headed for the shack. She had the chance in her hand, in the phone she was gripping for dear life, to finally make Connie Jansen pay dearly for all that she'd ever done to her and her sisters. Just in case she was right, and she believed she was, with all of heart, she would call Amy on the way to the shack. She would ask Amy to contact Adam as soon as possible and ask him to meet her at Connie's.

She dialed Amy's number knowing that she would wake her but hoping that she wouldn't mind once she heard what Kallie had to say.

The phone rang six times before Kallie heard Amy whisper, Hello? Hello?"

"Amy, it's Kallie. I'm sorry to wake you up. I know it's late."

Amy was obviously confused. "Kallie? Why are you calling me from the back room? Wait. I don't understand. Where are you?"

"Please don't get mad. I left you a note in case you woke before I got back but I see now that you didn't get up. I borrowed your car and went to Oscars Bar. I had to see Connie."

Amy was quickly awakening and understanding what her sister was telling her. "What? You are where? Why are you there, Kallie? What's going on?"

"There's so much I have to tell you, but it has to wait for a minute okay. I need for you to either contact Adam and ask him to meet me at Connie's or you can give me his number and I'll call."

"Adam? I don't understand…"

"Amy, I know I'm not making sense right now. I know you just woke up and none of this would make sense even if you weren't half asleep. I promise to fill you in later but for now, I need Adam to meet me at the shack. Trust me when I tell you that it's important."

"Okay, but are you alright Kallie?"

"I am better than I've been in an awfully long time. Please don't worry about that. I just need Adam to meet me out there as soon as he can, okay?"

"Okay. I'll call him right now. Please be safe and come back as soon as you can to tell me what the hell is going on!"

It had started to drizzle rain when Kallie left the bar. As she turned onto the unpaved road, close to the shack, the sky opened and a hard, driving rain fell.

"Great! Not the ideal night to be wandering around in the woods!" Kallie grumbled. "Then again, I guess it's never an ideal night for sneaking around in the backwoods of Maine."

Rain or not, she was going to see what her mother was up to. If she knew that woman like she felt she did, she would head straight to the woodshed or wherever it was that she had put Albert. Kallie didn't care if she caught pneumonia out in the chilly rain if it meant catching that evil woman with her hand in the cookie jar.

As she approached the turn off for the shack, she saw the beat-up jalopy of a truck pull out and drive off down the road. Whatever drunkard Connie had talked into bringing her home was leaving. That meant Connie was already home. Kallie planned to park the car, turn on the flashlight app on her phone, and creep down the path.

At first there was nothing but pitch-black darkness that eventually gave way to a feint light from the shack windows as she approached. The woods were dead silent. If there had been anyone around, she would have been able to hear them. Sound carried through those woods at night, especially when the air was heavy with precipitation. Maybe she'd been wrong, and Connie was too drunk to run around the woods checking on her secret? Maybe she had passed out. Maybe Connie didn't have Albert there on the property? Could it be true that she'd seen too many true crime movies? Her gut told her none of those scenarios were true. Rather, her gut was screaming that her mother was guilty, and it was past time for her to be held accountable.

As she passed by the "mountain" of old appliances, she heard the wooden screen door to the shack, slam shut. Someone had left the shack and Kallie's money was on Connie. She turned off the light to her phone and stood perfectly still next to an antique wood stove and held her breath. A heavy sense of Deja vu' swept through her body. All at once she realized that the dream she'd been having, was playing itself out before her very eyes. Except it wasn't a dream any longer. She no sooner realized that she'd been in this exact scenario before when she heard the sound. Again. Metal against rock. Rock against metal. Kallie continued to stand in the dark, completely still. She felt like she was back in the dream that had haunted her since she'd come back to Maine. She wasn't asleep this time! She was wide awake, hiding in the dark, in the woods. And someone else was out there too. Digging into the hard, gravel ground.

Kallie's eyes adjusted to the dark and she could see clearly. Connie was digging into the gravel earth, just like the night she'd witnessed twenty-two years earlier. Only this time she was digging up her father, not burying him.

Kallie willed her mind to stop her hands from shaking. She knew it was not the time to be scared. She was not that ten-year-old child anymore. She was not powerless. She was a strong grown woman, and she would catch her mother in the act this time! She had to! Connie wasn't going to get away with murdering her husband. If it were the last thing she did on earth, Kallie was going to see her mother pay for a crime she'd committed.

She quietly crept to the side of the woodshed, just out of the light that shone from the doorway. She leaned her head around the corner of the building and saw Connie bend down and retrieve something from the hole she had dug.

"There you are! You old bastard! Your oldest snot childs been nosin' around. Tellin' me how she's got proof I did somethin' to ya! Ha! Looks to me like ya still where ya was last time I seen your sorry, worthless, soul! I knew she was lyin' but I had to be sure."

Kallie turned on the video recorder on the phone and slowly took a single step forward. Connie's back was to her as she looked down at the ground. She was holding something in her right hand while her left was resting on her hip.

"Come to think of it, I guess I been pretty lucky no one's found ya 'fore now. Probably wasn't too smart of me to put ya in the ground to begin with. I think it's time we be havin' ourselves a little cremation ceremony. Ya know, just in case that nosey brat does ever come lookin' for proof. Yep. That's what we need to do." She took a swig from the bottle she had set on the ground beside her. "Now don't go nowhere ya hear? I'll get me a nice lil fire goin' and we'll fix ya up right nice." She let out a loud cackle that filled the night air.

Connie began to whistle while she tossed kindling wood from the shed into the fire pit. Kallie took a step back into the darkness. Her heart was racing so fast that she was afraid Connie could hear it from where she stood. The rain had let up a bit and the fog began to appear, slowly moving in around the trees that surrounded the shack.

Kallie took another step backward to be sure she was out of the lit area. Slowly she put one foot down and then the other, being careful not to make a sound. Connie was about to burn all the evidence of Albert's murder! She'd need to get that on video somehow. She'd have to be quiet and remain unseen, but she had to get it recorded. It was the only chance she had at proving Connie's guilt. She would do whatever she needed to do to make that happen.

Kallie took a deep breath and exhaled slowly and silently. She knew she'd need to figure out a plan before all the proof was turned to ash. Her hands began to shake either from the cold dampness or from her nerves, she wasn't sure which. She knew it didn't matter the reason, really. Being out in the woods, stalking the crazy woman who gave birth to her was reason enough to make a sane person afraid. If she didn't get her teeth chattering and give herself away, she'd be okay.

She reached into the pocket of the windbreaker she had borrowed from Amy, looking for something to wipe the droplets of water that had fallen onto the phone. It too, was getting wet and the last thing she needed was for it not to work when she was ready to use it. As she shifted the phone from her right hand to her left, it dropped to the ground with a thud.

Connie stopped in her tracks and Kallie's heart felt like it was going to stop. She looked right in the direction of Kallie's hiding place and said, "Hello? Who is out here? Brandy? That you? Get your ass back in the house!"

Kallie heard the footsteps approaching her. There was nothing left to do but run. She'd have to run ahead of Connie and hide in the dark somewhere. Somewhere she wouldn't be seen. Connie had to know it wasn't Brandy who was hiding in the dark. Brandy wouldn't have run, and Kallie realized she shouldn't have either at that point. But it was too late for that now. She had been careless and now risked getting caught because of it. The woman was preparing to burn the bones of her husband that she murdered twenty years earlier, she'd have no problem burning two bodies. Whatever she did, Kallie knew she couldn't let Connie find her.

She remembered the vivid dream she'd been having since coming to Maine. The giant Maple wasn't far from where she was. It had hidden her from someone in her dream, hopefully it could hide her from Connie in real life. She tip toed to the old tree and quietly leaned against the rugged bark. She breathed as softly as she could. In the beam of a flashlight, her breath would be visible, so she leaned her head forward and breathed into her jacket.

She could hear the footsteps coming closer then stop. Connie was shining the flashlight all around her but thankfully didn't go around to the other side of the tree. Kallie felt relieved when she heard Connie walking away from her. She would stand in that spot and not move a muscle until she knew for sure that Connie was far enough away.

She peered around the tree, moving only her head. Connie must have put more wood on the fire because the forest lit up with the orange light. Somehow, she was going to have to get closer to the shack again without Connie spotting her. She had to somehow record Connie before she completely turned Albert Jansen to ashes. Kallie knew she had to move but her feet stood still.

As she stood against the protection of the old maple, she willed herself to move. She would walk softly sneaking from one tree to the next until she was back at the woodshed. She knew what she had to do but she couldn't convince her legs to move from where they stood.

Just as she was ready to make the move, a hand from behind the tree, grabbed her shoulder and another clamped tightly over her mouth. The urge to run took over her body as she struggled to get away from the grasp of whoever was behind her.

"Shhhhh. Kallie, it's me, Adam. Don't say a word. Not a single word. I'll move my hand from your mouth, but you have to be quiet."

Kallie nodded. Thank God it was him! She turned to face him as he came around the front of the tree. She could see his eyes in the glow of the large fire that Connie had built.

"Adam. Thank God it's you. I thought…"

"It's okay. You're okay. She doesn't know either of us are here right now. You're safe."

Kallie had never felt so much relief in her entire life. "She's dug up my father's bones and has lit that fire to burn him. I was going to record her with my phone so I could have proof of what she's done. I dropped the phone and she heard it, so I had to run. We've got to stop her from destroying the evidence, Adam!"

"Did you see the body, Kallie?" he asked.

"No. I saw her looking into the hole she dug and was talking to him like he was alive. Telling him how he was going to have to be cremated because I was nosing around asking questions. Please, Adam, you've got to stop her!"

"And I will, but you have to stay right here. I'm going to record what she's doing and when she gets ready to burn the bones, I will step in. In the meantime, Kallie, promise me you will stay right here."

"I promise. Thank you, Adam and please be careful!"

Kallie watched as he quietly crept to the side of the wood-shed where she had been hiding earlier. Connie went to the hole in the ground and returned to the fire with shopping bags filled with bones.

As she tossed a bag into the fire, Adam heard her say, "So long ya cheatin,' good for nothin,' waste of life! I won after all! Ain't no man gonna tell me he's leavin' me for the town tramp and think for one hot minute he's gonna walk outta these woods! Ya shoulda known that! But you was too busy bein' in heat like the scroungy dog you was! Guess I get the last laugh after all, Al!"

Adam stepped into the light of the fire and said, "I don't know, Connie. The last laugh is reserved for someone else entirely, I believe. You, however, are under arrest for the murder of Albert Jansen."

Connie jumped clear off the ground at the sound of Adam's voice. She tried to run, but the broken, drunk woman was no match for him. He lowered her to the ground where he put handcuffs on her and led her out of the woods and into his cruiser.

Kallie walked to the woodshed after they were out of sight. Grocery bags full of bones scattered the ground. She knew she should feel something that resembled sadness to see the man who had helped to give her life, lying in pieces on the ground. But she didn't. She didn't really know the man and what memories she did have, were not good. His biggest accomplishment in life was that he helped to create four daughters. That was all he had ever done for her. Or for her sisters. For that, she allowed herself permission to not feel a drop of sadness. He didn't deserve her sympathy. He had met his demise at the hand of the woman that he chose over his own children. Somehow, in her mind, that seemed like a fitting end to his life.

As Kallie walked back to the road and to Amy's car, she said aloud, "Lord, please forgive me if I enjoyed the sight of that woman in handcuffs, just a little too much. She did have it coming though. You have to give me that much, right?"

CHAPTER TWENTY-FOUR

Kallie drove back to the cabin and try as she may, she couldn't get the smile off her face. She had barely turned the key to the off position when the passenger door flew open. Amy was in her pajamas demanding to know that her sister was okay.

"Jesus, you jumped me, girl!"

"Sorry. No! Not sorry. I've been worried sick! Are you okay? What is going on Kallie? Why did you need the police?"

Kallie smiled, which annoyed the hell out of Amy. "Why are you smiling? I don't see anything to smile about! I've been pacing these floors worrying about you. You wouldn't believe the things that have gone through my head. The scenarios I've imagined…"

Kallie reached for her sister's hand. "Okay, take a deep breath sister. Let's go inside and make coffee. I'll catch you up on everything."

Five minutes later, Amy placed a cup of coffee in front of her sister. "Okay, there's your coffee. Now, out with it. I can't take this a single second more!"

Kallie laughed but Amy was not amused. "It's not funny sis! Tell me what is going on, please!"

She didn't really know where to begin. "I don't know where to start, Amy. So, I'll just play this for you."

Kallie placed her cellphone on the table and played the video of Connie talking to Albert's bones as though he was there in the flesh. Halfway through, Amy's cellphone went off. It was Adam requesting that Kallie email him the recording that she had taken against his advisement, as soon as she could. Amy still didn't understand how Adam was involved. She hung up and continued to listen to the recording.

All at once, it was perfectly clear what was happening. "Oh my God! Oh my God, Kallie! Are you kidding me? Did I really just sit here and listen to Connie talking to the remains of our father?"

Kallie smiled. "Oh, you most certainly did!"

"Lucinda was right! All these years she claimed that Connie was involved somehow, and she was right! And Adam? He confronted her with this?"

"Confronted? Oh, I'd say he did! He was in the shadows watching her as she was about to burn all of Albert's bones in a huge bonfire out by the old woodshed! Seeing him arrest her, and the look on her face as he stepped out from the shadows was something I'll never forget! I so wish you could have seen that, sis!"

"I don't imagine she went quietly. Wow! Kallie! I just can't believe this is really happening. All the lies, the hurt, the suffering that she is responsible for is finally, in some strange way, finally being accounted for. She's finally having to pay for at least one thing that she's done in this life to hurt someone."

"That's how I feel too, Amy. We can't ever erase the pain and hurt that she inflicted on us while we were kids. And I think we've done all right at working through those things as adults. But this does make me feel that at least, for this one thing, she's having to answer for her wrongdoings. That almost makes everything her daughters have gone through, worth it."

"I agree. I wish we had never lived the lives we lived with her. But we wouldn't be half of who we are today if we hadn't had to claw and fight for everything we wanted in this world. I feel a sense of peace knowing she didn't get away with something, yet again."

Kallie agreed. "I wonder how Ginger and Brandy are going to feel about this? Do you think either of them will be surprised at anything that's happened in the past month?"

Amy wasn't sure. "I don't know. I think nothing will surprise Ginger. I think she's never put an ounce of trust or faith in Connie and half expected that mother could be responsible for about any terrible thing. Brandy is another story altogether. I don't know what goes through her head. She's too much like Connie to care about things one way or another I think."

They sat at the table discussing Connie and their sisters as well as their lives back at the shack, for hours. Before they knew it, Adam was home. They had talked for five hours straight but it seemed like an hour. He gave them each a hug and hoped they were doing okay considering what had occurred. Amy made another pot of coffee, and they continued their conversation.

"I don't suppose either of you have turned on the television or read the news on your phone?" he asked.

They both shook their heads. Kallie asked, "Why? Did the paper find out what's going on already?"

"Well, it's a little more than that. A search warrant was issued to search Connie's property, about an hour or so ago. Somehow or another, the mainstream news media got wind of it. Just before I signed off duty, dispatch told me that there's a circus of news outlets, local and national, moving in outside of the shack."

Kallie and Amy both had their mouths wide open. "Are you serious?"

Adam nodded. "It's not every day that a wife is caught holding the bones of her dead husband and preparing to toss them into the fire! Just the fact that she killed him twenty years ago and has been living with his bones buried on the property is newsworthy enough. The fact that she dug the bones up all these years later, to burn the evidence, well, that sells a lot more papers! Big news!"

"Oh wow! I never even thought of that!" Kallie smiled. "I wonder how Brandy is going to deal with that?"

"I was just thinking the same." Amy added. "Do you think we should go over there and see if she's okay or if she needs help or something?"

Kallie doubted that Brandy was going to want to see the likes of her.

"You know her better than I do. But I do know her well enough to know that I am the last person she's going to want to see."

Adam interrupted, "Ladies, it's not my call but I don't think either of you want to be in the middle of *that* craziness."

They knew he was right. It had been quite an unexpected night for both and when Kallie said she was going to try to get a minute of sleep, Amy agreed that it would be good for her to try also. Adam too, for that matter, since he had worked the night before and was having all he could do to keep his eyes open.

As Kallie lay in bed, the last thing that went through her mind was seeing Connie Jansen escorted from her property, in handcuffs. A warm feeling of satisfaction spread throughout her body as she fell asleep.

CHAPTER TWENTY-FIVE

Kallie opened her eyes a few hours later when she felt someone beside her in the bed. She pried her eyelids open; surprised to see a familiar face. He was sitting on the edge of the bed not saying a word but smiling as he looked down at her.

"Cam? What in the...? Honey? Is that really you?" she squealed.

Cam reached for her and held her in his arms. Kallie could not believe he was there.

"How did you find this place? What about London? How did you get here?"

Cam lightly pressed his finger to her lips. "Shhhh. No talking now. There's time for that later. Right now, I need to spend some time with the most incredibly, loving, caring, giving, beautiful, woman I have ever known. I've missed you so much more than you could possibly ever know babe."

Before she could respond, Cam's lips brushed against hers in a hurried, fevered way that told her exactly how much he had missed her. He held her close until there was no distinguishing between whose heartbeat belonged to who. This was as it had always been with the two of them. No matter what was going on in the world, their love and support of one another was the one thing they both knew they could always count on. They were each other's refuge and each other's inspiration and that was never something either of them questioned. Kallie's world felt right now that she was lying beside her soul mate. It didn't matter a bit what was going on outside that room, she was in heaven for the moment.

Hours later, heavy pounding at the bedroom door awoke them from the peaceful sleep they had drifted into.

Kallie spoke, "Yes? Amy? What's wrong?"

Amy flung the door open but had her eyes squeezed tightly shut.

"I'm sorry! I hope I didn't interrupt anything! Are you decent?"

Kallie laughed. "We're decent. You can open your eyes!"

Amy apologized again for the interruption as she sat down next to Kallie on the side of the bed.

"I just thought you'd want to hear this. I just heard this online."

Amy played the news brief from her phone. It was the familiar voice of Channel 5's national correspondent, Jake Jones.

"Connie Jansen, a lifelong resident of Somerfield, Maine, was arrested last evening for murder. The arrest came after alleged proof surfaced to indicate that Mrs. Jansen was involved in the disappearance of her husband, Albert Jansen, back in 1975. A search warrant was executed at the home of Mrs. Jansen where cadaver dogs found the remains of a man expected to be Mr. Jansen. Mrs. Jansen is being held at the Somerfield County Jail without bail at this hour. This story will be updated throughout the day."

Amy took Kallie's hand into her own. "And she would have gotten away with it for the rest of her life if you hadn't come back to Maine. I don't even know what to say to you, Kallie. I owe you; we *all* owe you, a giant thank you! We have watched this woman lie, cheat, and steal for her entire life and get away with everything she did. Not this time! Not this time!"

Kallie hugged Amy and a river of tears flowed between them. It was as though there had been heavy, invisible chains around them both that they never knew were there. The sense of relief they felt was overwhelming. Neither of them knew how to put into words what they were feeling but they quietly understood that no words were necessary. Their messed-up world was righting itself before their very eyes and they were honored to be witnesses. They were equally grateful to have the comfort of one another. Although they were fortunate to have loves in their lives, there was no one who could understand what they had been through, except one another.

Kallie giggled. "I was just thinking that I came back to Maine to take care of Maddie's things. To gather up a lifetime of memories that belonged to her. Turns out, Maddie was looking out for me once again. If not for that newspaper clipping we found at her house, we would never have known anything about Albert going missing. She knew we would come across it and pursue it. One last gift from Maddie."

Amy nodded. "She's your angel and I think she always will be."

Tears of gratitude and love for the woman who had shown her how to be a good, kind, loving person rolled down her face. Amy was right. She could feel Maddie in the room with them even as she wept tears of love and gratitude for her. With no idea what her life would be like from that moment on, she knew it would be forever changed.

EPILOGUE

For the first time since 1975, three of the four Jansen girls were together again. Ginger and her husband had accepted an invitation to the cabin for a barbecue and a reunion of the sisters. As soon as Ginger heard about their mother on the national news, she'd phoned Amy. If the surprise of her mother murdering her father hadn't been enough, she certainly was surprised to learn about Kallie. Even more so to hear that Kallie had been staying with Amy.

Brandy was also given an invitation for the reunion but hadn't responded one way or the other. None of the girls expected that Brandy would ever want anything to do with them again after Connie's arrest. And Kallie was certain that she would never speak to her again once she learned about her involvement in the arrest of their mother. Brandy had lived a lot longer with Connie than any of them had and they feared that she had become too much like her to ever want anything different out of life.

Krystal declined the invite to join them but thanked Amy when she called. She appreciated that they had included her but said that she was happy with her life just the way it was. None of them blamed her at all for feeling that way. She had lived her entire life without them in it. Without sisters and without a father. She and Lucinda were close and that was all Krystal cared about. Still, Kallie mailed her the sister bracelet to do with whatever she decided. She had already given Ginger's to her and was happy to see a smile as she thanked her with a hug.

The girls were enjoying a meal made by their husbands when a car drove up the driveway. Much to everyone's surprise, Brandy got out of the back seat and paid the driver. All three sisters sat with their mouths open in astonishment. This was certainly not something anyone had expected to happen. She looked nice. She had new jeans, sandals, and a button up blue women's blouse on. Amy stood and walked down the steps toward her sister. Kallie and Ginger were right behind her.

Brandy spoke before any of them had a chance. "If the invitation is still open, I'd like to get to know you all again. I haven't had a drink since mother was arrested and I don't intend to ever have one again. I plan to make a life for myself without her. A real life. I'd like for all of you to be part of it if that's something you would like also. I know I haven't always done the right things or said the right things, but I would like to be a better me. I don't even know what that looks like, but I'm willing to find out."

Amy, Ginger and Kallie looked at one another and then at Brandy. They had a group hug and a long cry among themselves. Kallie retrieved the bracelet she had for Brandy, who cried uncontrollably at the kindness from her sisters. A lot of healing would be taking place among them all in the days to come. They had been given a gift of family that Connie Jansen had done her damnedest to erase. But they were in control now. Connie was where she deserved to be. No one would be looking back but instead moving forward. Life was about to present them all with a gift that no one could ever take from them again.

In the days that followed, Kallie and Cam stayed on with Amy and Adam until they knew it was time to get back to Virginia. Kallie decided that Maddie would be happy if she didn't sell the house to a stranger. Instead, she gave Brandy the key and welcomed her to her new home. A decision that Kallie knew Maddie had been part of all along. In hindsight, it all seemed so perfectly clear how Maddie had set the stage for so many good things to come for the Jansen girls.

THE END

ABOUT THE AUTHOR

Karla lives in the beautiful state of Maine with her husband. She worked for several years in property management and social services before leaving to write full time. She is currently working on her next book.